To Tom

Good luck with the
writing!

CRUISE OF
THE UNDEAD

LAURA A. HANSEN

All rights reserved, including the right of reproduction in whole or in part in any form. This book is a work of fiction. Any references to historical events, real people, or real locales are used fictitiously. Other names, characters, places and incidents are the product of the author's imagination, and any resemblance to actual events or locales or persons, living or dead, is entirely coincidental.

Copyright © 2012 Laura A. Hansen

First Edition

Printed in the USA.

For information on purchasing this book visit
www.CruiseOfTheUndead.com.

ISBN-13: 978-1478165934

ISBN-10: 1478165936

To Charlie and Jack with love

ACKNOWLEDGMENTS

Writing this book has been an adventure. The book, and the journey of writing it, were only possible thanks to the patience and enthusiasm of my family. Charlie and Jack provided the spark of inspiration that was nurtured into a blaze to sustain the story. A thousand thank yous are due to my husband and partner in life Dave for many careful reads, good suggestions, and unwavering support. Thanks to Paul Thayer for editing and encouragement. I am also indebted to early readers of the book including Alex Welch, Porter Holmgren, and Vicky Virador. Thanks to Maddie, Christian, Matt, and Lois Hansen for reading all the way through Kids' Week. Thanks also to Jason Steele of www.filmcow.com for the use of the Charlie the Unicorn song. iPhone® is a trademark of Apple, Inc.

CHAPTER 1

DAY ONE

My parents have put me in a floating cage. Prisoners have more space than I do.

I lie on my bed and frown at the low ceiling, head and feet pushing up against the rails. It's the first day, and I'm already bored.

"Get up and do something. Go to the pool," Mom says.

There'd be more room in here if she went back to her own cabin.

Some winter break this is. "I'm out of here," I say, rising from the bed, and slipping through the narrow space between my mom and the built-in dresser. I snatch my cruise ship ID off the dresser as I pass, and scowl at my stupid, smiling picture on its front. I head down the hallway and thread my way between the cabin boys making up the rooms. A little Chinese guy named Johnny is our steward. He waves cheerily up at me as I pass. I hold back a sneer and keep going. At fifteen, I'm too old to be entertained by his arrangement of stuffed animals on our beds and too young to have any real fun. I'd rather be anywhere else than crammed into this stupid ship.

I slouch onto the first empty elevator and hit the button for the bottom deck, farthest away from _her_ suggestion of sunshine and pool. The door opens onto a chilly carpeted lobby with an advertisement for the matinee performance of "Illusionist Harry MacGuffin" posted on the dark paneling. In the poster, bright blue eyes glow in a fiercely grinning face. Cheesy music comes from the dark and almost empty theater. Totally lame, but no one will bug me here.

I wander in, sit in the last row in the back and crank the sound up on my iPhone. I pull one bud from my ear to hear the announcer say, "Ladies and germs, boys and gems, welcome to the Paradise Theater for a special demonstration of fantastic feats."

Ugh. I replace the ear bud and slouch lower in my seat, eyes half closed.

Music blasts my eardrums as a much older version of the magician from the poster shuffles onstage. His tuxedo hangs loosely over his gaunt frame, and the stark spotlights etch every wrinkle on his face. His hands in their white gloves are steady, though, and he gestures smoothly as he speaks from center stage. He conjures a blue-tinged fog with his hands. As he continues to swirl his hands, the mist rises like a tide from his ankles up his legs. It swallows the stage lights and leaves only a dim glow. Harry's arms rise higher, until he's nearly invisible behind the fog. Despite the dimming of the spotlights, his shadow looms ever higher and darker on the wall behind him.

Suddenly, he slashes his arms down and flicks his fingertips out, whisking the dark mist from his figure. The sudden light reveals the younger, tall and strong-looking man from the poster.

Hmm. Not bad.

After several sleight-of-hand tricks, Harry takes off his hat and waves it around. He pauses, still for the first time. He stares at the audience with his sharp teeth bared. He reaches into the hat. This must be the part when he pulls out some stupid rabbit. His mouth is a round O, though, as his hand emerges gripping the tail of a huge rat. The rat twists on its tail and latches its teeth on Harry's hand. He flails his arm to shake off the rat, but the teeth are dug deep. Red seeps onto the white glove. Harry's scream echoes through the auditorium.

The overhead lights come on, and the magician contorts alone on a dusty stage.

My eyes widen, and I say, "Now *that's* something you don't see every day."

I switch off the music and stand for a better view as a crewman in coveralls enters. He has a canvas sack that he slips over Harry's arm, neatly capturing the rat. Still it takes several yanks, accompanied by wails from Harry, before the rodent lets go. As the crewman carries the rat away, Harry frantically pulls at his bloody sleeve. Out comes a bouquet of flowers seemingly from thin air, except it's coated in glistening red.

Nasty.

Now he's got my attention as blood drips on the stage, and all the little kids in the front row scream and scatter.

I stay in my seat as the activities director climbs onstage and curses Harry. Harry can't seem to talk without his hands. His arms flap wildly as he protests. Blood splatters the director, the stage, and the front rows of seats. The magician's eyes roll wildly under the stage lights.

I watch until they leave, then pause another minute, staring down at the empty stage. Finally, I walk out of the theater alone.

CHAPTER 2

Standing in the lobby, I shiver in the chilly air. Maybe a chair by the pool isn't such a bad idea. When the elevator arrives, I press the button for Deck 12. After a quick ride up, the elevator opens to a warm breeze and noisy chatter. I step out onto the deck.

"Charlie! Charlie!" I turn toward my brother's voice and squint through the glare.

Jack whips a football at me from the wave pool. It thuds into my stomach. He's tall for his age, like me, and even in his swimsuit he looks like he's wearing shoulder pads. His brown hair is slicked to his head, and his blue eyes squint against the sun.

"Throw it here!" Jack yells. A small boy with blond hair and a bigger kid with fiery red hair converge on him. I pass the ball to Jack. They tackle and dunk him just as a wave hits. Their wrestling in the churning water creates a monster splash that soaks me from Nikes to shirt.

"Ugh, Jack, you jerk!" I shake the water off.

"Hah-ha, come and get me!"

"Hey, Charlie, come get your swim suit," my mother calls from a lounge chair.

"'Kay, Mom, thanks. Look out, Jack, I'm gonna kill you." I find a bathroom, change, then race back to the pool and cannonball into my brother's face. The lifeguard shrills her whistle.

"Eeeeeh," screeches a group of girls lounging on the deck—a bunch of bikini babes taking it all in.

I lift my brother, throw him into the water, and then dunk the red-haired munchkin dude and then the mini-munchkin dude, though gently because he's little. They splutter, huddle up to plan a counterattack, then split up to come at me. I circle to the left to line them up. Easier to take 'em down one at a time. Soon it's an all-out brawl, with water flying. Most of the girls scatter, except for one girl my age I can't help but notice. Instead of running and squeaking, she stays put and watches, wearing a little smirk.

"Charlie, knock it off! You're annoying everyone," Mom cries. Only now do I hear the lifeguard's shouts.

"Okay, okay. Settle down, midgets," I say.

Jack says, "Charlie, this is Nolan Hoskinson and his little brother, Truman."

Leave it to Jack to make friends before anyone else has time to sort out where the bathrooms are.

They are wiry and smaller than my brother. Nolan is maybe twelve, like Jack, and his little brother, Truman, is the same size as my six-year-old cousin.

"Hey, little dudes," I say.

"This is my neighbor, Savannah Smith," says Nolan, gesturing at the blond girl poolside.

"Hey, Charlie," she says casually.

"Hey," I say, in my deepest voice.

Maybe a cruise is not so bad. I lean against the side of the pool and watch Jack retrieve the football and pass it.

The football flies over my head, so I jump for it, showboating a little as I splash down into the water. After coming to my feet, I shake the hair from my eyes and line my shoulders up for a throw, giving it just a little extra. Jack catches the pass and throws it quickly to Truman before Nolan can tackle him. A whistle sounds loudly. The lifeguard on the platform shouts at us again, then jumps down to scold us for playing rough and splashing people.

I glance at Savannah. Her hair is plastered to her head, and water drips into her eyes. "Sorry, did I splash you?"

"No. Not at all." She looks up and holds out her hands. "I think it's starting to rain."

The sky is blue behind her, and up above the sun shines hotly down. Not a cloud in the sky.

I look back at her, then tilt my head and raise my eyebrows. She shrugs and heads for a lounge chair. I follow and climb into the lounge chair next to her with as much cool as I can muster.

This is starting to get interesting. Savannah is seriously cute with her wet hair and a red bikini. What do I say to a girl this hot?

A crew member with an accent strolls by, scans our ship IDs and goes off to bring us sodas.

"So, you're neighbors with them?" I tilt my head toward the brothers.

"Yeah. Our families came on the trip together. I don't know anyone else here," she says.

"Me neither."

Savannah grabs my ID and studies the picture. "Longish blond hair, green eyes, narrow face, nice smile," she says. She looks over at me. "Very photogenic."

I've got nothing to say. I think my brain has melted. I twist the paracord bracelet on my wrist nervously.

"I wouldn't have picked you as a jewelry person, though."

My face feels hot. I say quickly, "I wove this myself from parachute cord. Useful for a zillion things." Too late I realize she's joking.

Luckily, I get sucked back into the ball game before it gets too awkward.

My stomach's rumbling by the time we go. Before we leave, we make plans to meet up tomorrow.

We go to our cabins and get ready for dinner.

Once in the dining room, we're seated at a large table with several older couples. As the adults talk, Jack and I mostly just twiddle our thumbs. The rest of the evening is one boring blur.

The meal lasts way too long. There's too much food, too much noise, and nothing interesting going on.

After the long meal, we walk back to our rooms. I can't wait to climb in my bunk. The steward Johnny has folded our covers neatly back and put chocolates on every pillow. Sleep calls me. I drop into bed and conk out.

CHAPTER 3

DAY TWO

When I get up the next morning, the cruise ship thing doesn't seem so bad. I find things I want to do in the ship's newsletter that was pushed under our door during the night. Wish I had my friends here to hang out with, but Savannah is my age and she seems cool.

The sunny dining hall is busy when my family arrives for breakfast. The smell of bacon and pancakes makes my mouth water as I wait in line. I fill a plate and enjoy the food, but I can't help but be bothered by all the porkers going back for thirds and fourths at the buffet table. Kind of makes me sick to my stomach. Sheesh, like my brother. Look at the fat little piglet. I think he's on his fourth donut. Across the table, my mom munches on some super crunchy cereal. Dad slurps his coffee.

This is too much. I need to get out of here.

I turn to my brother. "Jack, let's go down to the theater. There's an Alfred Hitchcock movie on." Somewhere cool and quiet sounds good. Plus, I love Hitchcock.

"No, dude, I want to shoot some hoops upstairs."

"All right. Hey, Mom, I'm going down to see a movie."

"Okay, Charlie, see you at lunch," she replies.

Don't people do anything but eat on this ship?

As the elevator descends, I'm reminded of the gruesome magician of yesterday.

Today outside the theater, the magic show poster has a big red *Cancelled* written over it.

Once I get in the theater, I find it again mostly empty. I sit down to wait in the same back row as yesterday. Good to be far enough back that I'll avoid the blood, 'cause a place like this probably has no idea how to clean up properly. That's why there're so many flu epidemics on cruise ships. That and the fact that thousands of people crowd for weeks into hamster-sized cages.

The curtain rises, and the screen comes down. Apparently I'm right under the projection booth because I can hear the guys up there.

A high voice says, "Phil, did you hear about Harry?"

"Sure, he made a terrible mess of the theater yesterday, and guess who got to clean it up?" replies Phil gruffly.

"That's right; you were the one who caught the rat. Pretty handy that was. What'd you do with it after you got it in the bag?"

"Took it down to the crew observation deck and threw it overboard. I was glad to get rid of it."

"Those things have diseases."

"Especially that one. Harry claimed it came from that hellhole Del Diablo. He was down in the worst of the slums before we left, looking for some suckers to play cards with."

"Prob'ly planning to cheat somebody out of their paycheck again," says the other voice, just as the movie starts.

The opening to *Dial M for Murder* rolls. I've never seen this one.

A door creaks up in the projection room and a new voice speaks. "Hey, Phil, aren't you creeped out by this movie? Don't you know there's a corpse on board?"

These guys are really annoying. I can hardly hear the film.

"Wha-ut?"

"Yeah, Harry passed away in the clinic. Doc says he got some infection from that bite. Captain says we're going to have to keep him until our next stop the day after tomorrow. Apparently they're moving big coolers of ice down to the clinic for him."

"Oh no, too bad for him. And on Christmas eve, too." Phil sounds a little guilty now.

"Yeah, too bad for us. Anybody gets sick will have a big surprise."

All of a sudden, I've lost my taste for Hitchcock. I leave and go back up to my room.

CHAPTER 4

Jack is already in the cabin, throwing a rubber ball against the wall and talking nonstop, like always. Dad sits in our room, too, doing the crossword in the only chair and talking baseball with him. Jack winds up for a pitch, which hits the wall next to me.

"Steee-rike one!" he shouts.

"Knock it off, Jack," I say.

He winds up again, one leg up, right arm back and then over the top with a big follow-through step. *Whomp!* It hits an inch from my face.

"Stee-rike *two!*"

One more windup. I grab my pillow like a bat, and hit the ball back at him and out the open door. I tag the bathroom door, sock feet slipping on the carpet, and then the heavy wood door to the hall.

"That's a double," I say.

We leave the room. He pitches the ball down the hall at me. It's barely wide enough for him to do his whole crazy

12

windup. I hammer the pitch with the pillow, and he catches it off the glossy paneling.

"You're out!" he calls.

"Dad, am I out if he catches it off the wall?"

"No, you can't catch it off the wall," Dad says distractedly.

"Dude, you missed it."

"I got you," he insists.

He throws the ball. "Oh and two."

"Dude, that was a wicked throw."

He pitches the ball again, and I nail it, but it hits Dad as he steps out of the room. "That's it, you're done. *Done*," Dad shouts.

"Dad, did you see it curve?"

"Yeah, yeah, but you hit me."

"Yeah, but did you see how hard I hit it?"

"That's enough, you monkeys."

"Okay, but just one more pitch." Jack throws the ball. I smack it hard as I can.

The ball hits our steward on the ear as he comes around the corner, then ricochets from the steward's ear into the wall lamp. The glass globe falls off and shatters on the floor.

Uh-oh.

Johnny looks seriously unhappy and almost drops his armload of towels.

"You boys not throw ball in hallway. You boys damage ship and be trouble!" he shouts.

"Sorry, Johnny, we won't anymore," I say. Then to Jack: "It was your throw."

Jack shrugs.

"He'll pay for it," says Dad and turns to me. At six-three he's still got four inches on me. His hand clenches the back of my neck and spins me around. "You're going to apologize and make arrangements to pay for the damage. Now, go clean up your mess."

Johnny frowns at us and goes into the laundry room.

"Guess we're lucky you left the bat behind," says Dad to Jack as I start throwing broken glass into our trash can.

"I've got my bat. It's under my bed," says Jack.

Dad groans. "Why? When would you use a baseball bat on a cruise?" He points him toward the mess. Just like always, Jack somehow manages to look busy without really doing anything.

After I've picked up all the glass, Dad marches us around the ship. How humiliating. The purser on Deck 5 takes my name and address after I give my apology for the third time. Jack just mumbles and doesn't have to pay, even though it's *all his fault*.

"Let's get out of here. I'm hungry," says Jack.

"You're always hungry, you fat little piglet."

"Charlie, apologize," says Dad.

"Well he is."

"Charlie."

"I'm sorry I called you a fat little piglet. You're a little boy, a *little* little boy, not a pig. Don't know how I could have been mistaken."

Jack punches me in the stomach, but I see it coming and tighten my abs first, so it doesn't hurt.

"Jack!" says Dad.

I smile at my brother viciously as I cover the two steps between us, but Dad blocks me with an arm. "Let's go get some lunch, boys."

We take the elevator up to eleven to the buffet. Jack sits next to me at the table, so I get up and move. I stare out the window. Dad sits between us with his tray of food. After a while he says, "When I was little, your Uncle Buddy and I got into all kinds of trouble together. Did I ever tell you about the time he broke my arm?"

Dad drones on, but I tune him out. Outside the window, seagulls dive-bomb the swells. *Whack!*

From the corner of my eye, I see Dad lift his elbow and let his wrist and hand dangle awkwardly. He says, "He was scared and took off running. I walked into the house bawling, and Grandma almost fainted. Of course, they were crazy to know what happened."

"And?" I say.

"And I didn't tell. I never told her or Pop that Buddy broke it," he says.

I stare out at the empty ocean.

"What happened?" asks Jack.

"No TV for a month."

"That's child abuse," says Jack.

"I never ratted Uncle Buddy out, and you won't either, right? He's my brother and my friend, no matter what," he says, looking at each of us in turn over his glasses.

I sigh loudly. "Okay. We get it, Dad." I stand up to leave. "Jack, let's go meet the others."

CHAPTER 5

The midgets and Savannah wait for us by the rock-climbing wall. I look up the thirty feet to the top—my kind of challenge. I grab the largest pair of climbing shoes from the rack and put them on.

The instructor is tiny and Asian-looking, a couple of inches shorter than Jack. She says to us, "Put on a harness and shoes." She holds out a rope that's attached to the harness around her waist. "The rope is your safety net, so no worries. Just have fun! Use your legs as much as possible, and try to keep your weight off your hands. You can let go, and I'll lower you to the ground, or you can climb down. Any questions?" She looks around at each of us, bouncing on her toes and nodding. "Right then, who's first?" she continues brightly.

I step up, and she clips me into the rope. Keeping my weight on my toes, I lean into the wall. Like a spider, I climb to the top and ring the bell. I pause for a look around. I'm directly behind the bridge in the bow. The climbing wall is the highest point on the ship. The decks below are a warm brown, intersected with the bright, flashing rectangles of the pools.

People move constantly within the encircling rail, while beyond the railing the empty ocean stretches out.

I glide back to the others as the instructor cheers, "Fantastic job!" This little chipmunk's been drinking too much coffee.

Nolan steps up to the wall.

"Hey, Jack, you better not do this since you're scared of heights," I tell my brother as we watch Nolan clip in and start up the wall.

He gives me an angry look and puts climbing shoes on.

Nolan has no problem at the bottom, where the hand- and foot-holds are close together. Truman and Jack stand next to me as we watch him climb. He's fifteen feet up, about halfway, where the wall curves outward and it gets a lot tougher. He holds on with all four limbs as he hangs below it. He's stalled out.

"Nolan, move your left foot out to the side. Now up a little," coaches the instructor. He moves his foot, searching blindly for the foothold. "That's it, a little more to the left. Up a little. That's it, there it is," she says.

Nolan stretches, but his left foot doesn't quite reach. Now his right foot slips as well. Nolan hangs by his hands with legs dangling. He's pretty strong for a munchkin, and tries to pull his feet back up to the wall. He can't do it, though.

Nolan slips from the wall, and there's a gasp beside me. He falls a couple feet before the rope catches him. He slams into the wall and then rests against it, feet holding him upright. The instructor hauls him up a few inches, past the overhang, and Nolan grabs on again. It's tough for him now. The distance between handholds is farther apart, but the instructor keeps the rope taut and half pulls him over the rough spots. He doesn't give up, and smiles back at us as he rings the bell.

After Nolan comes down, Savannah steps up and clips in. Beside me Jack says, "Charlie, do you think that rope always catches you if you fall?"

I turn. "Depends on who's holding the rope."

He frowns. "How's it work?"

"The rope's attached to a pulley at the top, and it's held by the instructor on the ground. If you fall, she'll keep you from dropping very far."

"But the instructor isn't very big."

"Jack, it doesn't matter. It's a pulley system. No wait." I change my mind. "You're right. You're way fatter than she is. There's no way she can hold you." He walks away, talking to himself.

I watch Savannah climb. She's lean and flexible, with long legs that give her more reach, and gets to the top without too much trouble. As the instructor lowers her gently, I call, "Jack, your turn."

He walks over to the instructor. "Look at that. You're about the same size as her. No wait, I think you're taller," I say. I bet he'll chicken out.

The instructor clips him in. She's talking quietly to him, and he nods. He walks over to the wall and looks back at her.

"I've got you," she says.

He takes hold with his hands and starts up tentatively. Huh, he's actually doing it. Only five feet off the ground, but he's still going.

Hmmm. No, I was right. He's about eight feet off the ground now, and isn't trying anymore.

"You're okay, just move your foot up," calls the instructor.

"Come on, Jack, you can do it," says Nolan.

"I can't. My feet don't fit," replies Jack.

Yeah, right.

"Okay, no problem. Let go of the wall, and I'll lower you."

Jack twists around. "Are you sure?"

"Don't look down. I've got you. I promise," she says.

"Okay." Jack lets go with his hands, and the instructor eases him down a little at a time. He walks his feet down the wall to the ground.

He unhooks the harness. "It wasn't so bad. I'm glad I went."

"Yeah, you were like three feet off the ground," I taunt him.

"Nuh-uh. How high was I?" he asks the instructor.

"You were a good eight or ten feet up," she says.

He looks up. "Halfway?" he says.

"Not quite," she replies. "You think about what I told you. You can get past this fear."

"My feet didn't fit, otherwise I could have kept going," he says.

"Try again another day," she says.

"Yeah, when your feet are smaller," I mumble.

Truman bounces up and down next to the wall, "I wanna try. Lemme go!"

The instructor bends down to help Truman, and Jack and Nolan run off for some munchkin-sport. Savannah and I stand alone on the deck.

I look at her, "You really zipped up that wall," I say.

"Yeah, you too. Are you in sports?" she asks, watching Truman as he grabs onto the handholds.

"Uh, well, I play a lot of golf, I guess, and spend a lot of time outdoors, shooting or camping."

"I've never played golf. It's crowded where I live."

"You seem in pretty good shape. What do you do?"

"I'm in track. I run the mile."

"Pretty fast?"

"Well, I like it, so that helps."

"I was in track last year, but it's not my thing."

"Oh, yeah? There's a track up above us." She glances past Truman on the wall to the open deck that circles above our head. "We could work out together sometime."

"Yeah, sure," I say. Absolutely no way am I going to get on a track with her.

"Want to run tomorrow?"

"I guess." No. I mean no.

"Okay, I run in the morning. You want to meet before breakfast, maybe seven?"

She's really cute, and how can I say no, but, seven in the morning? "Uh, maybe a little later?"

"Come on, don't be a wimp," she says.

"All right," I agree.

What? Did I really say that?

After that, the conversation sort of dies out as we watch Truman finish up. I'm not sure I can trust myself not to say something stupid. The three of us walk down to our rooms. She waves as I leave them at Deck 9.

"See ya," I call.

That night, Christmas eve, we have a family dinner to celebrate the holiday. It's okay, but not anything like it would be at home.

CHAPTER 6

DAY THREE

The day starts off way too early. When my iPhone alarm rings at five to seven, I'm cocooned in my bunk with the blanket over my head. I roll out of bed and punch my brother awake. He just looks too comfortable. There's a bulging Christmas stocking at the foot of my bed. I dump it and look over the goodies. There's a nice Swiss Army knife, which I pocket, along with a gift card for the ship's store. I stash all the rest of the loot, mostly candy, in my nightstand for later.

I throw on shorts and ride the elevator to the track on the main deck. I can't believe I'm doing this.

The sun is too bright as I squint up at it, even though the morning is still cool. But anything for a lady. I peel my eyes fully open to see her long legs coming toward me in some skimpy running shorts. Savannah has her hair pulled into a blond ponytail. Her eyes are a sparkly green in the sunshine even though her face is set in its usual cool expression.

21

"Good morning, Charlie," she says brightly.

"Uh-huh."

"So, I guess you're not a morning person?"

"If by morning you mean noon, then yeah, I'm a morning person."

"Hmmm."

We fall into step on the track. She starts jogging slowly, and I lengthen my steps, keeping to a slouchy walk beside her. She speeds up, and so do I, now at a fast walk. She looks sideways at me. I smile. She speeds up until I'm speed-walking, with arms pumping. Another sideways look at me, and I respond with a cheerful grin.

Savannah snorts a laugh and comes to a stop, facing me. "We don't have to do this if you don't want to," she says.

"No, no, I'm good."

"Ready to do some real running now?"

"Yeah, sure, show me what you got." We fall into step at an easy run.

"By the way, that's a very nice laugh you've got," I say.

Savannah snorts again but covers it with a cough. She speeds up, and I stay with her and then pull ahead a step. Savannah speeds up some more, and so do I. After a lap or two of this, we are at a dead run, or at least I am. Savannah still looks like she's cruising. I realize I'm in trouble 'cause this girl may be seriously fast. I can keep up with most anyone at my school, but she's something else. I give it one more push, and she easily keeps pace. Savannah turns to me with a big grin.

"Go for it," I say.

I coast to a stop as she takes off, really racing now. I sit down on one of several big crates labeled "Fireworks" to watch as she flies away from me. Quick as anything she's back around and slows to meet me.

"Wow," I say.

"Thanks." She smiles. "I was second in state last year."

"How 'bout some breakfast, speedy?"

"Sounds good."

Christmas music drifts from the dining room. Mistletoe hangs above the entrance.

Awkward.

Did Savannah see it? I veer to the side and make a detour to the hand sanitizer next to the door. I turn back to find her watching me from under the mistletoe.

"There's a lot of viruses on cruise ships," I say. "People get all sorts of nasty stuff, diarrhea and vomiting, and it spreads to everyone on board.

She replies, one hand on her hip, "I don't think that happens very often."

"You hear about it all the time in the news."

At the buffet, we line up with our trays behind a crowd of old folks, breakfast smells wafting back at us.

We shuffle along, filling our plates with pancakes and fruit. There's a fountain of chocolate milk, and I fill a glass. As Savannah looks ahead at the line, I grab some smelly fish off the buffet, its head still attached, and place it on her tray. She looks down, and her eyes widen before she glances back at me. She sticks out her tongue, and I smile.

Once we're at our table we dig in. I'm happy to see the tidy way Savannah eats. I can't stand to watch, or listen to, noisy eaters. All around us, fatties head back for seconds and thirds and chow down with their mouth open. Gross! I focus instead on Savannah, and tell her what happened with the magician yesterday. She's a really good listener, and the story comes out funny and creepy at the same time.

I don't think I've ever talked to a girl this long. Feels pretty good. We linger a long time at the table. When it's long past time to go, we walk out side by side. As we leave, Savannah suddenly grabs me around the neck, reaches up, and kisses me on the cheek.

Still close, she points at the mistletoe above us and says, "Merry Christmas!"

I manage a mumbled "Merry Christmas" in response, my cheeks hot enough to roast chestnuts.

CHAPTER 7

I leave Savannah at the elevator and wander off to see what I can get with my Christmas gift card.

My head is strangely fuzzy. I can't help thinking about that kiss under the mistletoe, and I soon end up lost in an area marked "Crew Only". The hallways are even narrower than ours, and the ceilings are low. Some off-duty crew members hang out here, reading or playing cards. Through open doors, tiny cabins are visible, each with two beds crammed in. Spanish music and then Russian-sounding voices float out of open doors. Several people look up with surprise when they see me. At the very end of the hallway a windowed door opens onto an outside deck. Several uniformed crew members walk toward me. I take the door to the outside, thinking it may lead me back to the passenger areas, but the only walkway leads down and right back into another dimly lit crew hallway.

More steps lead down to what seems like a mechanical area. It's crowded with equipment and vibrating with engine noise, but surprisingly no one's there. After threading my way around metal pipes, I step through a heavy door into another vacant corridor, this one quiet enough that my footsteps are loud.

As I walk, another set of steps echo mine, although with a slower and uneven beat. Are they in front or behind? Better figure it out and get out of here before I get in trouble.

I search for a way out. Large work-rooms open off the corridor, some kind of communications room right next to a large carpentry and metalworking shop. I'd love to check out all the equipment, but the footsteps are louder now. I stand quietly, ears alert. The sound is harsh and hollow, with an eerie hitch and drag to the step. I turn around. The sound comes from somewhere behind me. I hustle ahead through the corridor, which runs straight for twenty yards. Almost at the opposite end, hallways branch open to the left and right. When I look backward, a dark silhouette fills the hall. After the mess with the broken lamp, I don't want to get in trouble again.

I take the hallway to the right, which curves around toward the bow. I'm feeling a little panicky now. Surely the ship can't be this big. Doors open off the hall on both sides. I glance into each, finding a jumble of storage rooms, but no exit. The same uneven footsteps sound behind me. Are they closer? I'm walking as quietly as I can, but my breathing is loud in my ears. At last, a red Exit lights up the door ahead of me. I walk through and quietly pull the door closed behind me.

I lean back on the door and exhale shakily. Where am I? Too quickly, the door cracks open behind me. I jump out of the way and turn.

A tall shape steps through and hovers over me. As the figure staggers toward me. The smell hits me first. He stinks like a rotten fish. He's filthy and soaking wet. Sheesh, dude, take a shower.

I can see his face now—it can't be! It's the magician, or else his twin brother, who towers above me. He stumbles forward, reaching out for me. His mouth sags open, his skin pale and bruised-looking. When he grabs my arm, a low and raspy "Ohhhhhh!" comes on his drawn-out exhale. The rank smell of his breath turns my stomach.

I stare, frozen, into his eyes. His blue eyes are glazed over with milky white film.

His mouth opens wide. He leans into me.

Waking from my shock, I try to pull away. He's got my wrist in his grip. He's pretty strong for someone so messed up. He reaches for me with his other, bandaged hand. I flinch back.

I open my captive hand wide, twist it up and clockwise around his hand, and break his grip.

I whirl and trip over a crate.

Cold fingers slide across my back. They catch my shirttail as I twist onto my hands and knees.

I scramble to my feet, jerk from his grasp, and run.

My footsteps are so loud I hear nothing behind me, but that doesn't stop me from imagining the worst.

I run until I'm back in a crowd.

Old ladies and silver jewelry fill the lounge outside the gift shop on Deck 5. By this time I feel like an idiot for running like a little kid. What's wrong with me? I'm frightened of some sick dude? What was I thinking, he was a ghost or something?

I need to get help so I head for the clinic on the third deck. My thoughts still race when I reach the clinic door.

It opens onto a reception area. The doctor and a nurse sit by the desk with coffee mugs in hand. Apparently there's not much business. No flu outbreaks yet.

The nurse rises, clipboard in hand, and approaches me. "What's the matter, sweetheart?" she says.

"There's someone very sick downstairs."

"I'll need the name and room number," says the nurse, indicating the chair in front of the desk.

I sit. "Uh . . ." I don't know how to start.

"What seems to be the problem?" asks the doctor.

"He looked an awful lot like that magician that got his hand bitten a couple days ago."

"What?"

"Harry the magician is limping and ill downstairs," I say.

I can see he doesn't believe me. "Not possible. Harry is, uh . . .Well, it just couldn't be him."

"Is Harry supposed to be dead? I heard some of the crew talking about it."

"Why do you think it was him?"

"He was wearing the same tux he had on stage two days ago." I'm dismayed to hear a tremor in my voice.

The doctor rolls his chair around until I'm knee to knee with him and puts his hand on my shoulder. He wears a white turtleneck under his doctor's coat and looks steadily into my eyes. Oh, jeez, we're going to have a heart to heart. You can always tell when adults get all serious on you that you're in for it.

"A lot of people wear tuxes on a cruise ship." He looks at me like I'm the sick one, and I don't know what to think now, so I don't say anything. "Did you see him get hurt in the theater? Was that upsetting to you?"

"Uh, yes, I mean no."

"Tell me your name, son."

"Charlie."

"Charlie, I'm going to be honest with you here."

"Okay."

But he doesn't say anything. The silence stretches on. The clock on the wall ticks loudly. What? Give it to me straight, doc. Harry's a serial killer? The ship's haunted? I'm not a real doctor, I just play one on TV?

Finally, he says, "Harry did die, and I'm very sorry that you had to hear about it."

"What did he die of? Was it an infection from that rat bite?"

"No, no. He lived pretty hard, and it was just his time." He pauses again. "I'm sure you can understand that it would not be good to share this with the other passengers. Everyone is here to enjoy themselves, and we want them to continue to."

"Yeah, okay, but are you sure he's dead? Maybe he got better and he's out there needing help."

The doctor's gaze shifts to the examining room next door and then back to me. A pool of water has seeped under the door, and he flinches when he sees it.

"No, son, I'm quite sure," he says.

"Could you check? Just to be sure? Maybe he isn't quite dead." Maybe he isn't quite dead? Jeez, did I really say that? Mentally I roll my eyes at myself.

"Charlie, I'm afraid you're getting a little overexcited."

Suddenly I see the magician onstage again in my mind, and I'm utterly certain it was him in the corridor. My hands go cold, and my mouth is suddenly dry. It must show on my face, because the doctor takes my arm.

"I think we need to get you back to your parents."

Like I'm two. Like I'm in need of a babysitter. Time for a quick recovery.

"No, Doc, I'm fine. I'll get right back to my mom and talk this over." Like crap I will. But I *will* make a fast break for the door.

I head up the stairs. The doctor clearly thinks Harry is on ice in the examining room. What could have happened? It must have been someone else in the hall.

I wander up to the library and sit at a computer. I log on to the Internet and search on *Harry MacGuffin*. I find a bunch of publicity photos of him. He's got the same blue eyes and dark hair as I remember. When I see the smiling picture, I freeze. I close my eyes and concentrate on my memory of the man I saw below decks. I see Harry's mouth open and smell the awful reek. Yes! The teeth are unusually pointed, like a rat's. I look at the photo again. The same teeth. It's the same guy, no doubt about it. The doctor thinks Harry is in the clinic, but I just saw him below decks.

I spend the rest of the afternoon on my bunk, paperback spread open on my chest but my mind somewhere else. Why would they lie about him? By the time my mom rouses me, I'm restless and ready for action.

CHAPTER 8

Dinner tonight is one of the two formal nights.

Getting ready in the cabin, shirtless and looking into the mirror, I grin at my reflection and blurt out a laugh before I can stop myself. I wonder if I'll see Savannah at dinner. I flex my bicep and kiss it, then turn around and flex in front of the mirror.

The door to the room opens. "She is really cute, Charlie."

"Mah-um!"

My good mood drops away at the doors to the dining room. A blast of noise hits me before I enter—canned Christmas music competing with chattering voices. The huge room, bursting with people, looks like a Christmas store exploded. Fake Christmas trees loom in every corner, and pine branches and red ribbon cover the tables.

It's Christmas. I completely forgot.

The menu inside the door lists six courses, which is gonna take forever to get through. I glance around the crush of people as we enter but don't see Savannah. Jack grabs Dad's sleeve and points, and Dad asks the maitre d' to seat us with Nolan's family.

Jack and I sit on either side of Nolan and Truman. I slap hands with Truman as I sit. This is already promising to be more interesting than the last two nights, as Truman is sure to be entertaining. Or, at the very least, *teasing* Truman is sure to be entertaining.

An old couple, a guy with brush-cut hair and pumped-up shoulders, and his small, limp wife, also join our table for ten. The old guy shakes hands with everyone before he sits down next to Dad. His meaty hand clamps hard on mine. "Lars Thorwald," he says. I put some muscle into it so I don't get my hand crushed, but he just squeezes harder. Jerk. His wife smiles faintly past him at me.

White-jacketed waiters scurry around the room, delivering plate after plate of food to other tables. We seem to have three waiters, all from somewhere on the other side of the world where people have much better manners. The boss waiter bows to take my order, graying hair neatly smoothed back. Afterward, he smiles and backs away, then turns to point and speak angrily at his number two, a young guy with dark hair and unusually pale skin, who moves like he's underwater.

After the salads, we're stranded and hungry in the sea of diners for a long time. I don't know why they can't get the food to us quicker. We're all restless, especially Truman. Waiter number three stops next to him with an apologetic smile. Without speaking, he plucks Truman's cloth napkin from the table and folds it into a Santa hat. Bowing deeply, he presents it to Truman, who puts it on. The adults smile. Nolan hands him his napkin, too, and the waiter folds it into a swan.

"Hey, I'll take one," says Jack.

The waiter takes his napkin and starts folding it into complicated shapes. He glances at the adults, and then, holding one end in each hand, he steps behind Jack. He lifts the napkin over Jack's head and places it across his chest. When he pulls the ends apart, the napkin becomes a bikini top.

Jack looks down at it and laughs.

I laugh and point.

"Hey, Mom, look! I've got a bikini on," Jack shouts across the table, and all the adults look at him.

The waiter quickly creates a bikini bottom for Jack and says, "Now you ready for swim pool." Embarrassed laughter comes from our parents. Thorwald and his wife frown. We cheer and applaud the waiter.

All of a sudden, the room seems brighter. The punch line of my favorite pirate joke comes into my mind. "Hey, Truman, a pirate walks into a bar. He's a complete mess. Got seaweed in his hair. He's all wet, and he has a steering wheel sticking out of his pants. The bartender says, 'You look horrible. Do you know you have a steering wheel in your pants?' 'Aye,' the pirate says, 'and it's driving me nuts.'" I'm not sure if Truman really gets the joke, but Nolan laughs so hard that he snorts soda from his nose. Mom rolls her eyes.

"I've got one," Jack says, as waiter number two fills our water glasses with a shaking hand. "Truman, say knock knock."

Truman responds, "Knock knock." I watch waiter number two stop halfway around the table, his hand on the back of Dad's chair.

"Who's there?" says Jack.

Waiter number two leans over the chair, breathing hard, almost gasping for breath.

I watch Truman's look of confusion and surprise when he tries to understand what went wrong with that joke, then turn back to waiter number two again. He's still holding Dad's chair with one hand, his other hand holds a heavy pitcher of water. The pitcher droops, and then drops yet lower. Uh-oh. Iicy water sloshes onto the lap of Mr. Thorwald next to dad. The old guy jumps to his feet and shouts.

I don't know who to be sorrier for, the waiter or Thorwald, but I can't help but laugh.

Thorwald's khaki pants are soaked dark. He turns to the unsteady waiter and starts telling him off. Other waiters hurry to help. Dad rises, takes the pitcher from number two and gives it to one of the waiters. He puts his arm around the sick waiter and gently steers him away.

Thorwald points his finger at the departing waiter, muscles tightening along his square jaw. "Idiot!" he calls after him.

Nasty.

Dad and waiter number three help the sick man toward the kitchen. He's barely able to stand, so they half carry him out. The boss waiter shakes his finger and quietly scolds him all the way to the kitchen. Afterward, number three brings bread baskets to the table, smiling apologetically with teeth gleaming.

"What's wrong with him?" I ask, looking back at the kitchen door. "Is he sick?"

"No, no, he is unfortunately very lazy," says number three.

I don't think so.

When Dad gets back, he and the uptight Mr. Thorwald hold a quiet argument that they think no one else can hear. The top of Thorwald's silver brush cut hair shows as he stands to blot his pants with a napkin.

"Take it easy, it's clear he was sick," Dad says.

I turn to Jack. "Looks like Mr. Thorwald forgot his Depends."

Uh-oh, he heard me.

Thorwald looks up angrily. "You need to treat your elders with more respect," he says to me, then adds to himself, "You little brat!"

"Don't speak to my son like that," says Dad with anger in his voice.

"If he's your son, you need to teach him some manners."

"He's just a kid. He didn't mean anything by it."

"He shouldn't come into the dining room until he's able to behave himself. If you can't control him, then I'll have to speak to the maitre d'."

"Forget it. I'm out of here," I say. I throw down my napkin and leave them to it.

I stomp all the way back to the room. I'm so mad, I'm not even hungry anymore.

Merry Christmas on the cruise ship!

CHAPTER 9

A couple hours later, I'm still aggravated by the adults on this ship. That jerk at dinner was bad enough, but I can't stop thinking about the doctor and the way he spoke to me this afternoon. Somebody's lying about what's going on, and I'm going to figure it out. I climb out of my bunk and I go in search of my brother.

I find Jack and his new friends at the lighted basketball court. I'm in no mood to wait, so I snag the ball as it's passed and throw it as hard as I can toward the other end of the ship. As the Hoskinson brothers race to get it, I collar Jack and pull him over to the railing.

How do I say this without sounding like an idiot? "Jack, something's going on. That magician who supposedly died yesterday? I saw him this morning below deck."

"<u>Was</u> he dead?"

"No, sick and gross, but walking."

"I don't get it."

"He's supposed to be on ice in the clinic. I want to go see."

Before I can stop him, Jack heads for the elevator and calls to his friends, "Come on guys, we've got to find a dead guy."

The other two charge onto the elevator with us. I press the button for Deck 3, where the clinic is.

"What are you talking about? An actual dead guy?" Nolan asks.

"Ewww, gross," says Truman.

"Ewww, cool," says Nolan, then, "What's going on, Jack?"

"Charlie says he saw a dead magician walking around on Deck 2."

All three look at me. All I can do is shrug and tell the story again.

When the elevator doors open on the third deck, we cross to the clinic door. No light shines beneath the door. The clinic seems deserted.

"You guys keep watch on the elevator lights and the stairs," I say.

I kneel on the carpet in front of the door and pull out my new knife. I've seen this work in more cop shows than I can count. I slide the blade between door and frame and wiggle it. Does it work like in the movies? Maybe I've just got the touch, because yes, it does. The door pops open. I enter the clinic and sneak into the dark examining room. A medicinal smell overwhelms me. The floor is wet, and there's a large tub overflowing with ice in the adjacent bathroom. I bring up the flashlight app on my iPhone and leave the lights out.

I stand over the tub. I realize I really don't want to do this next part, especially alone. I shiver. Probably a good thing they keep this ship so cold. I set the phone on the counter so the light shines on the tub. I pull on a set of latex gloves from the box on the counter, then gingerly reach both hands toward the ice. I hesitate. What shape is he in at this point? I can't think about it if I want this done, so I plunge my hands into the ice and shovel it away from the end of the tub where you'd expect the head to be. I don't find anything, so I probe deeper.

I'm cold and wet to the elbows, but there's still nothing. I guess that's better than touching a corpse, but why would they lie about him?

I panic and start raking ice onto the floor. I dig all the way to the bottom, but there's no body there. No magician, so he's not dead. Or maybe they had him airlifted out after all. But why all the ice?

I run out of the clinic and grab Jack. "Jack, come and look."

He doesn't want to—can't blame him. He's only twelve. I try to push him in.

"I'll go," says Nolan.

We leave Jack and Truman in the hall. Nolan and I stare at the empty tub in the glow of my iPhone.

"There's nothing there," he says.

"Thank you, Captain Obvious."

"You're disappointed? You wanted to touch a dead guy?"

"That's not what I mean. Let's get out of here. There's nothing to see."

We all take the elevator back up and make for our cabins. Back in our room, I turn on all the lights. Jack and I climb into bed.

"Jack, I don't know what's going on."

"What do you mean?" He sounds sleepy already.

"Could they possibly have been wrong about Harry?"

"He's not dead. You saw him alive, right?" He pulls his pillow over his head.

"Why do they have a tub full of ice, and why did the doctor tell me he's dead?"

"So somebody took an ice bath. Turn out the lights."

"Yeah, I guess," I say and reach for the light switch, but I still don't get it. After Jack falls asleep, I lay awake thinking about everything that happened today. I have this bad feeling, and I can't shake it.

When I finally fall asleep, I dream about a corpse chasing me down endless ship's corridors.

CHAPTER 10

DAY FOUR

The next morning, I wake up early and don't feel rested. The clock reads seven thirty. I wander up to the top deck, just for the view, you know. Oh, yeah, and maybe someone else has gotten up early, too. I catch Savannah just as she finishes her run.

"No exercise for you this morning?" she says.

"Not this early, but my stomach is growling already."

"How about some breakfast? Be good to go early. I heard that some of the restaurants are closed because of some bug going around. A bunch of the wait staff have turned up sick."

"I knew it. What've they got?"

"I don't know, but two of the waiters in our dining hall last night keeled over in the middle of dessert and had to be carried away."

"One of our waiters got sick, too. I told you, there's bad stuff on cruise ships."

"You're paranoid."

"You're not the first to call me that. I was down at the doctor's office yesterday, and it was completely empty. If there's a bug, it must be spreading really fast."

After breakfast, I head down to the Deck 3 and take a look at the clinic. There've been reports of flu, norovirus, even Legionnaire's Disease on cruise ships. If there's something spreading, best to know early and be prepared. I don't want to get too close, but the change in atmosphere is apparent even before I reach the clinic. Patients overflow the small office, so many that they're lined up into the hall. Savannah was right, there is something going around. As I pass the open door, two things strike me as strange. First, all the patients are wearing uniforms. There are no passengers in sight. Second, all the patients have open wounds or bandages. It doesn't look like a flu outbreak at all.

How did all these crew members get injured? I need to get inside, but I don't want another condescending lecture from the doctor. I need some camouflage.

I find the boys in the library. There are shelves full of books, but everyone is using the computers. Jack and his friends play a video game on the Internet.

"Can you come with me, Truman?" I ask.

He hops up and comes over. "Sure, Charlie."

"What's up?" Jack says.

"Nothing. Truman and I are going for a walk." We head for the elevators, Jack and Nolan trailing us.

"If you're taking a walk, why are you waiting for the elevator?" says Nolan.

Truman and I climb in and I push the "3" button. Jack sticks his head through the door to look at the panel.

He holds the door open for Nolan. "They're going to the clinic." They get in, too.

"We already looked around last night, when we broke in. What's the point of going back?" says Nolan, as the elevator drops.

"There's something weird going on," I tell them.

"Charlie, you *always* think there's something weird going on," says Jack.

"Whatever. Come on, Truman," I say. I take his hand, and they all follow me out of the elevator. "Truman, you're going to act like you're sick so I can get into that clinic and take a look around."

Jack says, "Truman, act like you're drowning, and we'll carry you in."

"Go in the bathroom and get wet," says Nolan.

"Yeah, let's put him in the toilet," adds Jack.

"No way, I'm not getting in the toilet," says Truman.

"Okay, we'll just stick your head in the sink," his brother says.

"You guys aren't any good at this." I tell them. "Truman, put your hands on your stomach. You're sick to your stomach, and you think you're going to throw up, okay?"

He nods.

"Let's see your sick look," I add.

He puts both hands on his stomach and smiles up at me. Two teeth are missing in the front.

"No, that's not sick enough. Grab your stomach and moan. Don't smile," I say.

"Think about Brussels sprouts, Truman," says Jack.

He looks doubtful.

"Truman," says Nolan, "I'm gonna punch you if you don't start crying right away, and I'll tell Mom it's your fault."

Truman hugs his belly and wails convincingly.

"Wow, I think I see a tear," I say. "That's very good, Truman."

He smiles up at me again.

"Truman," says Nolan in a menacing voice.

More wailing from Truman.

"You guys stay here," I tell Nolan and Jack. I grab Jack's ball cap and put it on with the bill pulled low over my face. I carry Truman to the clinic door and pause to look in. We squeeze through the crowd at the door and edge into the room. We move toward the left, sticking close to the wall. Truman looks convincingly sick, but no one pays any attention to him.

It's like a horror show around us. Wounded people fill the small clinic. Each of the two beds has a patient, neatly bandaged but unmoving, their eyes glazed. Drops of blood speckle the floor. The doctor stands off to the right, so I drift toward the examination room on my left. I open the door. We slide through and I pull it closed behind us.

A motionless patient, eyes closed, lies on the only bed, but otherwise the room is empty. I set Truman down and put my finger to my lips. After pulling the door open a crack, I peer out at the main room of the clinic.

The doctor bends with needle and thread over a burly man in a greasy coverall, a chunk of meat missing from his forearm. Another man's cheek is ripped from eye to mouth. I pull out my iPhone and take some pictures. Strangely enough, we're the only passengers there. The injuries to the crew are to hands, faces, shoulders, and arms. I count the injured.

The room is quiet. No coughs or sniffles from anybody.

"Charlie," whispers Truman, much too loudly. I turn. He's looking at the patient on the bed. The young woman in a waitress uniform lies still, too still. I lean closer, watching her chest and face. She doesn't appear to be breathing. Is she dead?

Truman reaches up to pull her heavy dark hair off her face. "She's cold!" he squeaks. Her eyes snap open at his touch, eyes half obscured by a milky haze.

Truman cries out, and I stumble backward into the door. Truman is spellbound, frozen in place, mouth open and hand suspended in midair. She snatches his hand and pulls it closer. Her mouth opens, but no sound comes out. She's slipping his fingers into her mouth when I yank Truman away. He wails for real this time.

"Let's get out of here," I say, and open the door with my free hand.

At the sound, the doctor turns and sees me. "Charlie, what are you doing here?"

"I . . . uh . . . I —"

"We need to find Harry, son. I need to talk to you about him."

"Uh, sorry, I don't know anything about him, really. I thought you said Harry was dead."

"Get over here, kid, this is serious business." He reaches for me, but I dance back, pulling Truman with me. We dodge several patients to edge closer to the door,.

"Wow, doc, looks like the crew holds cage fights downstairs. What's up with all these injuries?"

"We're trying to find that out. I need you to sit down here so that security can come down and interview you."

I nudge Truman, who begins to wail again. "Sorry, doc, I've got to get him out of here." I take two steps closer to the door. We're only a few feet from the exit.

All around us the patients stir, and a man grips my shoulder.

"Let's get out of here!" I yell. I pick Truman up and run for the stairs across the lobby. Once on the stairs, I charge up two steps at a time.

"Charlie!" calls Jack, as he and Nolan thunder up the stairs behind us.

"Come on, keep moving." Truman whimpers in my arms as I run. We don't slow until we reach the library, seven decks up.

CHAPTER 11

I'm still breathing heavily as I log on to a computer. I glance over at Truman. His lips tremble a little. He hasn't spoken since we left the clinic. "It's okay," I say to Truman. "You're okay."

"What's going on?" says Jack.

"What happened to Truman?" says Nolan.

My fingers fly over the keyboard.

"Charlie!" Jack says, demanding my attention.

"Nothing. He's fine, just a little freaked out. There was some psycho in there."

Finally, I access the files I need and download them. I print a stack of pages, but Jack snatches them off the printer before I can get there.

"'Preparation for an attack,'" Jack reads out loud. "What're you doing? Are you hallucinating?"

"Bug off, Jack," I say, and snatch the pages from him. I pat Truman on the head and take off for my room to read. Jack tags along.

I sit at the desk and read. Jack edges up behind me to read over my shoulder.

"What the—? You have apocalypse on the brain, man. It's like a high school obsession."

I elbow him in the stomach.

"Ow!" he cries, and jumps back.

He sidles up behind me again.

"Knock it off, Jack. You didn't see what I did." I pick up the document, holding it close to my chest.

"OK, OK. Let me hear, though."

I glare at him in the mirror before reading out loud: "'Preparation for an attack. Step One. Identify the threat level. How many attackers? What's the terrain? What useful personnel and skills are available?'"

"What about one sick old magician and a bunch of cage fighters in the basement? Where's that fit on the doomsday scale?" he says.

I reply, "Shut up, dude, and let me read. 'Step two. Acquire necessary equipment and supplies. Useful equipment: Firearms' Hmmm," I murmur to myself. "'Axe or hatchet. . .'"

"I've got my pocket knife. Will that do?" asks Jack

"'Sword—'"

"How did I ever go on vacation without my sword? What was I thinking?" He slaps his forehead.

"'Matches/lighter' Check. 'Crowbar' Double check. 'Bug spray. . .'"

"Haven't seen too many mosquitoes out here on the open ocean," says Jack.

"'Survival books.'"

"No need for those. You've already got half a dozen memorized," he chimes in.

47

"'Bicycles—'"

"Where are we gonna get a bicycle on a cruise ship, and what the heck are we supposed to do with it?" says Jack.

"Bikes are the best mode of transportation during an attack, on land. They're silent, so they don't attract attention from the nonhumans, and they never run out of gas."

"Nonhumans! Charlie, you gotta be kidding. You don't seriously think there's some alien invader on board?"

"It's pretty far-fetched, but a lot of people have been talking about, and preparing for, the apocalypse, so I guess I'm not as surprised as I ought to be."

"So what, we're talking ET gone bad?"

"No, not aliens exactly."

"What then?"

I pause for a long minute. I don't want to say it.

"Come on, what?"

"The living dead."

His mouth falls open. "Huh?"

"Zombies, OK?" There's an edge to my voice.

"So, you really buy into that fantasy?"

"Well, maybe there's a reason for all the zombie mania going around."

"And on a cruise ship?"

"Listen bro, a cruise ship is the last place you want to be when under attack," I say.

"Well, then, it's a good thing that this is all just a delusion in your head, so I don't have to worry about it."

"Maybe," I reply. "We'll find out."

CHAPTER 12

I skip the lunch buffet, and instead spend the afternoon camped out poolside, watching for trouble. No sign of anything wrong up here. The tweeners and teens have claimed one section of the deck. Kids yell and splash all around me. I've got a lounge chair, my zombie preparation printouts, four pools to choose from, and a continuous stream of waitresses bringing me all the junk food and soda a guy could desire. Plus, it's got great scenery, as all the lady teens are out, too. Savannah lies in the sun when I arrive, but the lady vanishes before I get up the nerve to go over.

After a while in the sunshine, it's hard to take the invasion thing seriously anymore.

Around three, Mom swings by. "I'm going to the afternoon tea. I think you boys should come, too."

"Aw, Mom, I don't want any tea. I've already had lunch," I tell her.

"What'd you have?"

"Hamburger, fries, mango smoothie, and, oh, yeah, a big plate of broccoli and Brussels sprouts."

"Nutritious. Maybe you're right. You probably don't have room for anymore."

"Nope, full up."

"Too bad. It's the Death by Chocolate Buffet today," she says with a smile in her voice. "Chocolate cakes, chocolate cookies, chocolate pies, chocolate fountains . . ."

"Woo-hoo, death by chocolate. Let's go," sings my brother.

"Okay, I'm coming. Anything for *you*, Mom," I add.

When we get to the dining room, there's a long line of pudgy old people waiting to be seated, everyone eyeing the long table full of chocolate. There aren't enough servers, but we're finally seated at a table for eight near the wall. Mom chats with a little grandma next to her as the waiters serve tea.

"These are my boys, Charlie and Jack," Mom says. She turns to us. "This is Lois from Iowa, boys. Say hello."

"Hey."

"Hi."

"Hi, boys, it's nice to meet you. I've got grandsons back home about your size. I bet you're having a wonderful time. It's such an exciting way to spend Christmas break."

"Um."

"Yeah, whatever."

"Lois has a room down the hall from our cabin, Charlie. I told her you'd help her carry her things down to the laundry room. It's such a long way down the hall."

I roll my eyes. "Sure, Mom."

"Oh, that's okay. They've got so many things to do. They don't need to fuss around with an old lady." She smiles, then adds, "What grade are you in?"

"Uh, I'm a tenth grader," I say, "and Jack is in preschool."

"Preschool?"

"Uh, well, sixth grade going on preschool."

"You both look like really smart children."

"Smart and smart-alecky," mumbles Mom under her breath as the waiter finally indicates it's our turn. We grab plates, two each for my brother and me, and fill them to overflowing with chocolate cake, double-fudge brownies, chocolate éclairs, chocolate pie, and strawberries dipped in the chocolate fountain. A four-foot-tall carved chocolate goddess with wings towers above us. We sit back down and dig in.

"Watch this, Charlie." Jack dumps his tea in the potted plant and runs with his cup to the fountain. He shoves his cup under the stream and fills it with melted chocolate. He lifts the cup to his face and glugs down pure chocolate. "Ah, this is the life." He smiles a full-on chocolate-coated smile, complete with chocolate brown teeth.

Lois laughs into her napkin while my mom groans.

The room fills with chatter and the sounds of silverware on china. The tea reaches the point when people shift from greedy little chocolate piglets to overstuffed hogs. I'm a little nauseous myself and push my plate away. Jack, however, still gobbles chocolate cake. I'm ready to go and start eyeing the door when it opens from outside. Must be one last chocoholic.

It's the magician, Harry, who enters. I'm so sure he's *not* here for dessert. He walks awkwardly with an off-balance and stiff-legged gait. Hairs rise on the nape of my neck.

Harry's still in his black tux, the shirt now streaked with brown and reddish stains. One coat sleeve is ripped at the shoulder. The filthy bandages on his left hand trail on the carpet. My gaze skitters from his face, where the flesh dangles in gray shreds. My stomach tightens, the taste of chocolate turning sour in my mouth.

I elbow Jack and point.

"Is he dead or alive?" asks Jack.

"Both, I think, and that's a problem," I say grimly.

Harry bends toward the woman at the nearest table. His legs struggle stiffly to keep up. The plump lady has her head tilted back, and she laughs loudly. She grimaces with wrinkled nose at his approach, then twists to see him and screams. He reaches for her. She scrambles out of her chair. She backs away, but stumbles after catching her foot on her chair. Harry grasps her upper arm. He leans toward her. She stretches away from him. Harry encircles her back with his other arm. As he lowers his head to her shoulder, her scream sends ice down my spine. Harry's sick embrace presses her almost flat onto the table, nearly into the lap of the woman in the next chair.

The man to her left stands. "Get your hands off my wife!" he shouts. He stiff-arms Harry in the shoulder.

Harry slowly lifts his head and faces the man. Harry's mouth drips blood. Harry towers over the little man, who gallantly stands his ground. Harry grabs the man by the ears and lowers his head again. The little man yanks his arm back and makes a fist. He punches Harry under the jaw. Harry's head tilts back, and then drops. His face falls forward just in time to be slugged with a left cross. This time the punch is less effective. Harry pulls the man into a bear hug. The little man continues to punch as long as he can. When they're too close, he elbows Harry in the chest. Finally, he slams his knee into Harry's crotch. None of it has any effect. Harry buries his teeth in the man's neck.

"Ben!" yells the woman. A ripping sound echoes through the room. Blood spurts from Ben's neck. The woman screams wordlessly, a long and mournful sound that ends in desperate sobs.

Everyone else is shocked into silence. Other men jump up to tackle Harry. A waiter runs to help. Together they wrestle Harry to the ground. He bucks, then turns to bite them as well.

A tubby lady springs from her chair and grabs a large silver tray from the buffet. Chocolate candies scatter across the floor. She straddles Harry and plants her butt on his back. He collapses onto the carpet. She raises the tray above her head and grunts as she smashes the tray onto Harry's skull, putting her weight behind it. The blow makes a crunching sound. Harry goes limp. People scream and run for the doors.

Through the milling people, Ben is visible on the floor next to Harry. He's unmoving. His wife sobs at his side and holds a blood-soaked napkin to his throat. She's bleeding, too. A red and brown mess coats the carpet around them.

The crowd jams the exits.

Mom holds us tightly as we retreat to the doors with the rest of them. "Oh, my dears, I'm so sorry. Let's get out of here," she says. I can hardly hear her over the crowd.

People fill the lobby and elevators. We take the stairs instead and get out quickly.

"Are you okay, boys?" She looks stunned and distressed, tears in her eyes.

"We're fine, Mom," I say. I look at Jack, and he does look fine, mostly recovered from the shock.

"That poor man! What on earth happened?" she says.

I mumble under my breath, "He went to the Death By Chocolate Buffet," catching Jack's eye, "and he got what he came for."

CHAPTER 13

As soon as we can pry ourselves from our worried mother, I lead Jack to our room, close the door and lock it.

I turn to face him. "Jack, we've got to prepare for what's coming. Harry was a zombie."

Jack scoops up a Nerf ball from the desk and squeezes it. "He sure seemed like a walking-dead eating machine."

"Pretty much the definition of a zombie. He's dead now, but more will come."

"How do you know he's dead? Everyone thought he was dead before, but he came back." He dribbles the ball on the desktop.

"Smashing a zombie's head in is the only way to kill them. You heard the crunch. That lady got him pretty good."

"Don't think I'll ever look at dessert the same way," he says. "So what do we do?"

I pace between our bunks from the window to the door. "I think we've got another day before things really break loose."

"How come?"

"Well, the first day was the day Harry got bit by the rat. That must have been how he caught the zombie virus. He got sick fast, died sometime that night, and was roaming around again soon after. He probably started attacking people as soon as he woke up, not long before I saw him yesterday."

"So?" he asks.

"It can't have taken more than forty-eight hours from infection until reanimation."

"You mean zombification?" says Jack.

"All the crew members that were in the clinic this morning will be zombies in another day and a half. That's when it's going to get real 'Harry' around here," I say.

Jack groans but manages to smile, too. "At least we can still laugh about it."

"Nobody's gonna be laughing when those zombies wake up and start going at it. The infection will spread exponentially after that."

"What's that mean?"

"The zombies will multiply. If there's ten of them tomorrow, then the next day there will be a hundred and then a thousand the day after that."

He stops bouncing the ball, and faces me. "Whoa. Everybody on board will be goners before the cruise ends."

I grab his shoulders. "We've got to warn the captain and get off the ship."

"We'll be in port tonight. We'll have to get out of here then."

"We need to get ready. We may have to fight our way out."

"Do we tell Mom and Dad?" he asks.

"Yeah, but they won't believe us."

We leave the room to talk to Mom and Dad in their cabin across the hall. They sit together by the window. Mom is still talking about the death by chocolate.

"I think that man got bit by a zombie," I tell them.

Mom looks up at me. "Zombies aren't real, Charlie."

"They *are* real. This ship is infected. We need to make plans to get off the ship when it docks tonight or else they'll come after us. Right, Jack?"

I look back at him. He's sitting at the desk, chair tilted back on two legs. "Um, yeah, I guess," he says.

"They're just a fiction in books and movies," says Dad.

"How do you explain what happened this afternoon, then?" I say.

"Charlie, I'm sorry that you had to be there. That man was obviously disturbed. I wish you hadn't seen any of that," says Mom, glancing at Dad.

My father says, "I think you've been reading too many horror books."

"Dad, I'm serious. We need to alert the captain that there's going to be trouble. He needs to call for help and isolate anybody who may be infected. We need to get moving *right now!*"

"We're not going anywhere, and you are *not* contacting the captain," says Dad, his voice rising.

Mom adds, "I heard that poor man had a long history of mental problems. What happened was tragic, but he wasn't a zombie. Anyway, whatever the problem, I'm sure the crew will take care of it."

"Yes, the zombie crew will have everything under control in a couple of days," I mumble under my breath and head for the door.

Dad gets up and follows me, "That's enough, Charlie. I'm sick of your zombie talk. One more word about zombies and you're grounded."

"Okay, okay, I've got it!" I shout. "There's no zombies, and I can't say anything to anyone. I'll be in my room reading." I slam the door behind me.

Back in my room, I throw myself onto the bed and roll over to face the wall. Idiots!

Jack comes in and hovers over my bunk. "What are we going to do, Charlie? They're not listening."

"If I push any harder, they'll just ground me. And by the way, you were really helpful."

"We're not gonna let the zombies get us, are we?" He sounds panicky.

I roll over and look at him. He stands pale and tense in front of me. If I don't do something, we all could die. I'm not gonna let Mom and Dad stop me. "No, we're going ahead in spite of them. Call your friends, Jack. We'll tell them what's happening and see if they'll help."

He jumps, tension suddenly released in action. "Yeah, right, we need a *team*. We need a Zombie Team, and we need to take them all out," he says, his fists pumping with his words.

I raise my eyebrows. "Zombie team?"

"Yeah, that's what it's going to be, the Zombie Extermination Team," he says with enthusiasm.

He's all pumped now. He uses our cabin phone to call the others.

CHAPTER 14

"Mom and Dad are just across the hall in their room, so speak quietly."

"What's going on, Charlie?" asks Savannah as she leans back against Jack's headboard.

"Zombies are taking over the ship. You've heard about the death by chocolate, right?"

"Is that a joke?"

"No. Harry the magician got infected by a rat bite, died, and then came alive again. He's been attacking people, mostly crew members."

Savannah and Nolan look at each other.

"What are you talking about, Charlie?" asks Nolan.

"Zombies are multiplying on board. Right *now*. As we speak! Within a couple of days they'll take over the ship."

Truman shrinks back. "Zombies! What's zombies mean, Nolan?"

"I don't know what Charlie is talking about, Truman," his brother responds slowly.

I don't get it. Weren't they listening? I try again. "Zombies are taking over the ship. They feed on living humans. By tomorrow it won't be safe to walk the halls. Within a couple days, the whole ship could be taken. We need to move if we're going to save ourselves."

They don't look convinced. My voice tense, I try once more. "Zombies are spreading on board. They feed on fresh meat, on *us*, and we're trapped like rats in this ship. We need to prepare if we're going to save ourselves."

"What exactly are you planning to do, Charlie?" asks Savannah.

I can see from her face that she doesn't believe me.

"I'm planning to save us. Or at least I was."

I look at Nolan. He looks away. I'm pissed now. "Go ahead and get eaten if you don't believe me," I say spitefully.

Savannah won't meet my gaze either.

"Okay, fine. Just forget it."

I stomp into the bathroom and slam the door. There's nowhere else to go on this stupid ship.

I slump on the toilet lid, my face hot. I flick the toilet paper holder against the wall until it thumps and bounces back, then do it again. *Thump. Thump. Thump.* The murmuring of conversation reaches me through the door. Why don't they leave already?

Jack's voice rises and falls. I put my head in my hands and think about all the gruesome ways they could die.

I can hear Jack clearly now through the door. I ease the door open and peer through the crack.

Jack reenacts the death by chocolate. Harry shuffles forward, bites, bites again and goes down. Jack makes a convincing fat lady as he wallops his stuffed dog with his pillow.

He gets up but keeps talking, walking back and forth. Wish he'd give it up. It's useless, and I want to get out of this stupid bathroom.

Savannah studies my printout, and she and Nolan talk. Oh, crap. I'm stuck in the bathroom forever. I look like an idiot.

Jack comes toward the bathroom. I close the door and jump away from it. There's a knock.

"Charlie, we have some questions," says Jack.

What do I do now? "Uh, be out in a minute." I flush the toilet and turn on the tap. My face feels hot but looks pretty normal in the mirror. Stepping from the bathroom, I try to look casual.

"Could you talk to us about what you think?" asks Savannah.

"No way. You guys don't want to hear."

"If you'd just take the time to explain."

"Forget it." I grab my shoes from the closet.

"Come on. Do you want help or not?" she says.

I sit on the side of my bed and start putting my shoes on.

"Charlie, don't be a baby," Jack says.

"Leave me alone. If you want to hear, I'll tell you, but then I'm out of here."

I'm angry, but I start talking. As they listen without protest, I slow down to explain and talk them step by step through what's happened and the trouble I'm confident is coming.

Savannah looks especially worried as she leans toward me from Jack's bed. "We have to tell the captain. He can isolate the infected and stop it from spreading."

Finally. It's such a relief for someone else to believe me. I glance at Jack, sitting next to her. Thanks, bro. Maybe I shouldn't have stormed into the bathroom. No, they were jerks about it, but leaving the cabin would have been better.

I refocus. "It may already be too late. Down in the clinic this morning, I counted more than a dozen injured. All of them were crew members. Plus there's the two victims from the Buffet. By the day after tomorrow, they'll all be wandering around killing anyone they find."

Truman looks confused.

"Like this, Truman." Nolan staggers across the aisle, zombie-style, toward Truman, and tries to bite him on the neck. Is he making fun of me?

"Who knows how many more have already been infected. It's spread so fast among the crew that I don't see what the captain can do beyond calling for help," I finish

Savannah pushes Nolan away and puts an arm around Truman. "We should go to the captain together."

"No. We'll get more done by splitting up. Time is short," I say.

"We'll be in port this evening. We can get help then if the captain doesn't listen."

"If we have a fully functional crew, then yeah, but otherwise we could float around the ocean for weeks," I say.

"We've got to be prepared to survive until we get there," adds Nolan. Good, Nolan's on board, too.

"Yeah, the next port is Kiribati. We can only hope that there's someone who can help us."

"Okay, so what do we need to survive?" asks Savannah.

"Food, water, first-aid supplies, weapons, tools," I say.

"But the bicycle, what about it?" says Jack.

"Huh?" say the others.

"Very funny, Jack," I say.

CHAPTER 15

"Okay, let's get started on the list," I tell them. "We'll split up and prepare. I'll go talk to the captain." Truman looks scared. I meet Savannah's gaze. She looks scared, too.

"I'll get the food," Savannah says. She looks down at Truman. "Truman can help me. It'll be fun." He looks relieved and smiles back at her.

"You guys go down to the shop and get weapons and tools. You know what you need?" I ask.

Jack nods.

"We've got the list," says Nolan.

Jack grabs his backpack from under the bed, and I do the same.

I take the forward elevator to the top deck and exit into the lobby behind the bridge. From the far side of it, I can see through a window into the bridge, where half a dozen sailors work in front of large windows. They look out at the sky and sea. Their workstations look a lot like what you see in the cockpit of a plane, except for the steering wheel in the center of the room.

Cool. I move around to the entrance, but a crewman standing in front of the door stops me.

"Excuse me, I need to talk to the captain. It's an emergency," I say.

"No entrance to the bridge, lad," he replies.

"He's gonna want to hear this. It's a life or death matter. I just need a minute with him."

"Nobody gets onto the bridge," he says again.

I step back and consider him. The guy looms over me with legs spread, hands on hips and elbows out. His crisp white uniform is tight enough to show he's spent some time in the gym. He's got his hand over the pistol on his belt. There's no way I'm going through him.

"Look, the captain needs to know that the ship is in trouble. There's an infection spreading among the crew. It needs to be contained, and he needs to call for help. If you get that message to him, I think he'll want to talk to me."

"Captain's orders. Nobody gets onto the bridge, not even me."

"But Harry the magician was infected with . . . Well, it made him crazy, and he killed somebody. I was there. Anyone who comes in contact with him will be infected, too. The captain's got to know about it."

His blue eyes soften some, and he replies, "Look, lad. The captain knows all about it. Harry injured a bunch of folks, but the doc is patching them up. It's under control."

"Why can't I talk to him? It's more serious than that."

"The captain's not letting anybody on the bridge. There was an altercation up here earlier, and he got slightly injured. He's okay. Doc put a stitch in his hand, that's all it was. But now nobody but nobody gets in there."

"But he needs to call for help," I protest.

"They've already contacted authorities. Harry's on ice until we get back to port. He'll be taken care of. We've got things well in hand. I appreciate your concern, but it's under control. Why don't you go on back and enjoy yourself? There's no reason to think we'll have any more trouble."

"But . . ." I search for the right words to convince him.

"But nothing. You need to leave *now*," he says, and his gaze hardens.

I back off and plod downstairs, thinking hard. With the captain injured, it won't be more than a couple of days before he dies and reanimates. This could be a lot worse than I ever imagined. The whole crew could be taken before they figure out what's going on. We can't count on them getting us outside help. Not as quickly as we need it.

I change course and hurry to the computer room. I'll get on the Internet and sound the alarm. If I send enough emails, one of them will surely get to the right person.

When I reach the library, I'm relieved to find the room empty. I sit at one of the computers and open the browser. It's slow, and I fidget while waiting. I might explode if I can't get this done, and right away.

"Hurry up, come on," I say to the stalled screen.

Finally, the screen changes. "No Internet connection available," reads the message. Crap. I try again and then open the browser on the adjacent computer, too. Nothing. I glance around the room. Most of the computers have the same box open, with the same message. What's going on? I struggle with the computers, rebooting several of them and checking the cables, but no luck. I turn on my phone. "No data service" lights up the screen. No connection there, either. Feeling panicky, I stand stricken in the middle of the room and slowly pivot. What should I do now?

I tromp down the stairs to my cabin. Jack greets me, his face excited.

"Charlie, we got one! We were down in the workshop, when we heard moaning. We found the zombie in the hall just outside the workshop. Nolan shoved it in a room with a two by four. I nailed it with a blowtorch. There was a bunch of paper in there, and it all went up. Next thing we know, there's a loud boom and smoke coming out the door. Everything was burned up. The zombie wasn't moving, but Nolan smashed its head with a crowbar, just to make sure. Didn't we do good?"

"Are you both okay?"

"Yeah, we're fine. No blood or anything. It didn't touch us."

"Good. No, wait. This is a bad sign. They're reanimating quicker than I thought. I think the captain got bit today, too, and I don't think Harry could have done this much damage. That certainly wasn't Harry down there with you in the shop," I say.

"Nope."

"Just a minute. You were next door to the shop. What room was it that you firebombed?"

"Said 'Communications' on the door."

"Oh, no. The Internet's down. I bet the wiring that connects to the satellite got fried. Now nobody can call for help." My mind struggles to take this in.

"What about cell phones?" he suggests.

"No, our cells only work where there's wifi, and the system was down in the library. They don't work out in the middle of nowhere. No cell towers. Haven't you noticed?"

"Oh."

"You guys fried the communications networks, and the zombies are reanimating faster than I calculated," I say.

"Not good."

"We need to be armed if we're going to save our butts. I'm going after the firearms."

"What makes you think they have guns?"

"Oh, there are guns, you just need to know where to find them."

CHAPTER 16

I spend the rest of the afternoon on the skeet-shooting deck. You have to be eighteen to shoot, but I just act cool, and nobody says anything. It's been a while since I've handled a shotgun, but I'm soon back in form. I hit eighteen out of twenty clay pigeons on my last time up, and am the last to leave. I chat with the instructor as he cleans up. He stores the weapons in a lockbox in the adjacent office, and locks the key in the desk drawer. He latches the door behind him, and I say goodbye. I'll come back later when no one's around.

As I enter the elevator, I glance at the waitress in the short black skirt riding down with me. She looks strangely familiar. I shift my gaze to the light panel above the door. I sneak another glance at her. It's Savannah with a room service cart. She smiles and punches my arm.

"What happened to you?" I say.

"We sneaked into the laundry room," she tells me. "I found this uniform and got the cart. Truman's underneath." She pulls back the tablecloth, and Truman peeks out at me. I squat for a better look. Truman hugs a bin full of single-serve peanut butter tubs with crackers, with a box of cereal balanced on top. Savannah lifts the domed cover on top of the cart to reveal a pineapple surrounded by bags of M & M's.

"This is our fourth trip," she says.

"You've been busy."

"We have enough food for a month. Some in each of our rooms, just in case."

The elevator chimes at Deck 10, and we meet Lois, the lady from the Death by Chocolate Buffet, on the way to my room. She stops Savannah as we go by. "Dear, could you get me some milk and a small container of coffee? Oh, and maybe some of those good pastries from the buffet? If it's not too much trouble."

"Oh, yes, certainly, ma'am. What room are you in?"

"Ten twelve. And thank you, dear."

My gaze meets Savannah's. 'What's up with that?' we say silently with our eyes.

"Back in a minute," Savannah says as she leaves.

In our room, Nolan and Jack dump tools onto the pile that covers one bed. Bags and boxes of food fill the other.

"Sheesh, looks like you're stocking an army," I say.

"We wanted to make sure we had everything," says Jack.

"Guys, I think the captain's infected, and all communications are out. We need to talk to our parents again. No one should walk around this ship unarmed. If they don't believe us, they'll be attacked before they realize what's going on."

Nolan holds up a bunch of hammers. "Here, have a weapon."

I take the largest of the bunch, a small sledge hammer a little less than two feet long. I slip the handle under my belt.

"How 'bout you, Jack?"

Jack shakes his head and grabs his baseball bat. "I'd rather carry this." He ties a length of cord around the handle and loops it over his chest.

"Better if we stay put as much as possible."

"OK," says Nolan.

"When Savannah gets back, you need to go tell your parents."

I walk across the hall to Mom and Dad's room.

CHAPTER 17

I catch Dad as he goes into the bathroom and pull him back into the room. Mom gets her shoes out of the closet. "Can you guys sit down and listen a minute?" I say. Dad reluctantly sits down, perching in the front of the chair while Mom sits on the bed. I pace back and forth while I explain about the infection and how we need to protect ourselves.

Dad's face is tight as he looks out the sliding door. Mom watches me with one hand covering her mouth. I should have known. They don't buy any of it.

"No matter what you think, you've got to stay in your room," I finish.

"We were just on our way to the pool," says Mom.

"Dad, won't you at least go with me downstairs to see if what I'm saying is true?"

"No, I've had enough of this," says Dad. "Your mom and I have cut you a lot of slack lately because we know that you're going through a lot of changes. We're done with that now."

"You're making a big mistake," I say.

"Knock it off," says Dad.

"Whatever." I walk away.

"Charlie, get back here!" Dad hollers after me.

I slam the door on my way out.

Back in my room, I look around at the mess. There's so much stuff, there's nowhere to walk.

If I'm wrong about all this, I'm in big trouble.

Dad bursts through the door into our room. Nolan and Jack look up from organizing the tools. My dad's face bulges as he looks around.

My insides shrink.

Dad roars at Nolan with arm extended, "Get out, you! Now!" Then, to me, "What is all of this stuff?"

Nolan silently slips past us and leaves the cabin.

"We're preparing ourselves for—"

"Enough! You're committing crimes on this ship, stealing tools and food, because of some fantasy you're playing out in your mind!"

"Dad, no, it's not like that!" I say.

"You're going to gather all this junk up, and I'm going to watch you return it all with apologies. I'm ashamed of you. We've given you everything you ever could have wanted, and you repay us this way? I've had it. You're grounded!" He points at Jack and says, "You, too, buster."

Dad steps over our stockpile. He gets right in my face. "When I'm done with you, you're—"

Mom enters the room and says, "Dave, maybe he needs some help. He's a good kid."

"He's completely out of control, and it's affecting his brother, too," he says. "We're done with all this zombie crap."

"Dave, let me talk to him. Charlie, come over to our room." Pushing us apart, she says to Dad, "Charlie's no fool. If he says there's something going on, I believe him."

I look at her in surprise.

She leads me into the hall.

"I'm coming with you," Dad says, grabbing my arm. "I'm going to talk some sense into this kid." Mom pushes him back into the room. "No, you're not. Your temper's getting the better of you. Take a minute to cool down before you do or say anything you'll regret."

"All right, but Jack, move all this junk out of here. Double-time, kid!"

Jack picks up an armload of tools and looks at him red-faced.

"Get moving, buster."

Jack carries his load into the hall and drops it.

As Mom and I go to her room, Nolan stands in the hall. He stares at us, his face extra-pale under his red hair. Mom starts to pull me into her room but sees Lois struggling with her laundry, half of it dropping on the floor.

As Mom goes to help, Savannah comes down the hallway from the far end. She's running awkwardly while pushing the cart, her hair streaming away from her face.

"Charlie, it's starting!" she calls over the sound of the squeaky cart.

Johnny the steward chases her with a stiff, straight-legged gait. His body strains toward Savannah, legs unable to keep up, lifting him onto his toes. His awkward progress is surprisingly fast, while the heavy cart slows Savannah. Johnny's outstretched fingers rake the empty air behind her. They're almost to me. I pull the sledge hammer from my belt and step toward them.

Savannah rolls past. With both hands gripping the handle, I swing it over my head and slam it down on the steward's forehead. Blood splatters the ceiling. He topples chin-first onto the carpet. Mom gasps and squeals.

I stand there stunned, and slowly lower the sledge hammer. I turn to Savannah, "Are you okay?"

She gulps back a sob, then kneels and pulls Truman from the cart. She wraps him in her arms.

"Did you get any blood on you?" I ask, pulling Truman away.

"No. Let me see you, Charlie." Savannah looks up at me. "You look clean." Truman leans against her legs.

I look at my mom. "It's gonna be OK, Mom." She's pale, and her face is rigid.

"But—, my baby, what have you done?"

"Don't <u>call</u> me that," I say.

"But you killed him." Her voice is high and breathy.

"He was already dead."

Jack comes out of our room with another pile of tools. He looks at Johnny, and his mouth falls open.

"We're okay, but Mom's had a shock. Where's Dad?"

"He's still in there. We didn't hear a thing."

"We're going to have to do this without them." To Mom I say, "The ship's infested with zombies. We're going to need all that stuff." I point to the pile on the floor. "If Dad makes me take it back, we'll be defenseless."

She looks concerned. She reaches out for me.

"Yes, Mom?"

"Charlie, go to our room, lock the door, and stay put. We'll get you some help, maybe a psychologist if there's one on board." She rubs her forehead nervously.

"Okay, Mom."

"I'm going to talk to your father." She goes into our room.

I pick up some long nails from the floor. I grab a hammer from the pile and drive a nail at an angle through the door and into the doorframe above the knob.

"Are you crazy? What are you doing, Charlie?" exclaims Jack.

Mom rattles the doorknob, and then pounds on the door. "Charlie, Charlie! What are you doing?"

I hear her only faintly through the door. I put several more nails through the door.

Nolan walks toward us, staring at Johnny lying in the hall.

"Let Mom and Dad out," says Jack.

"I'm not going to let them screw this up. Dad's not going to listen. This is the only way. As long as they're quiet, they should be okay. We'll come back for them when we've got things under control or when we have more proof. Let's get all this stuff into their room."

"Charlie, you have to let them out. You can't keep them in there."

"No."

"You'll have to let them out sometime and then what?" asks Nolan shrewdly.

"You can't keep them locked up, Charlie, they're your parents," Savannah says.

"You have a bad temper," says Jack.

I face them. "There's no time for this. You guys need to convince your parents to stay in their rooms."

They protest, but go down to Deck 9 to talk to their parents. Jack goes with Nolan.

Lois still watches from her end of the hall. She's been folding her laundry for a *long* time.

I walk down to her.

"What should I do?" she asks.

"You know what's going on?" I ask.

"I've seen enough to be scared."

"Yeah?"

"Well, it seems quite unsafe out here. I was thinking I should barricade myself in my room for a while. Maybe you could show me what to do."

"Lois, you're a very surprising lady," I say. "I can do that. Do you need anything else?"

"Thank you, dear, you're very sweet. Can I get my coffee and other things?"

"Sure, Lois. We've got it all right here."

I get her the milk, coffee, and pastries, as well as sandwich fixings from where they're scattered in the hall.

Lois says, "I've also picked up a few books from the library. Do you know how long this all might last?"

"Nope."

Once we're done, Lois has got quite a little stockpile in there, with enough food and true crime books to last a week. I finish up with her and call goodbye.

"Goodbye and good luck," she calls through the door as Nolan and Savannah arrive.

"Where's Truman?" I ask.

"He stayed with Mom and Dad," Nolan says.

"Probably just as well," I say. It's going to get ugly.

"My parents will stay in for dinner and the rest of the night," says Savannah. "I took them dinner, a really *big* dinner and a bottle of wine and told them it was my treat. Date night."

"You lied," I say.

"At least you didn't nail them in their room," Jack says.

"No, they were delighted to stay in."

"What about yours, Nolan?" I ask.

"Got permission to stay overnight with Jack. They're staying in, too."

Savannah turns to me and says, "What about the other passengers?"

"Huh?"

"They need to stay in their rooms, too," she says.

She's right. There must be many old ladies nearly as nice as Lois, and none of them deserve what's coming. I realize I haven't given any thought to anyone else.

The others look at me.

"We'll do as much as we can safely do to warn people before we turn in tonight," I say.

Savannah nods.

It's the right thing to do. It's also the smart thing to do. The more people stay in their rooms, the slower the infection will spread.

CHAPTER 18

"The halls are no longer safe," I tell the woman in 1031. "Zombies from the lower decks will attack anyone left alive."

She slams the door in my face.

I turn to Savannah and shrug.

"No one's going to buy that," she says. "Your own parents didn't."

"Charlie, we've got to let Mom and Dad out," says Jack. He looks out of place, wearing a baseball jersey and shorts, with his baseball bat resting on his right shoulder.

"Not doing it, Jack. You heard 'em, they'll never believe me. You do the next one, Savannah."

"We'll just say there's a bad virus on board," Savannah says.

"I don't think it'll work," says Nolan. He points the sharp end of a crowbar at Jack. "Would you stay in your room 'cause I've got a cold?"

"Ha. Maybe it's the Bubonic plague," he replies.

"We just have to take the time to reason with them," adds Savannah.

"Dengue fever."

"The Ebola virus."

"Good one."

"Whatever," she says mildly.

"Take your pick. Bring the cart. Give 'em food if they'll take it," I say.

Savannah knocks on the next door. An older lady opens it. "Good evening," Savannah says. "Captain's orders are to stay in your cabin tonight. There's a viral outbreak on board, and it's very contagious. I've got some food in case you haven't had dinner yet."

"Oh, dear. What sort of outbreak is it?" She takes peanut butter and crackers from Savannah.

"Uh, they think it's Dengue Fever."

"Oh, my, that sounds awful. Why doesn't my phone or TV work?"

"The crew is working on it, ma'am. I'm sorry, but we need to keep moving."

"Oh, yes, of course. Thank you so much." She closes the door gently.

"Show off," I say. "It's only 'cause you're wearing a uniform."

"It doesn't hurt to be nice to people," she tells me.

"And lie to them."

Savannah turns to face me. "By the way, your brother's right. You need to cool off and think before you act."

"I'm not letting them out. Let it go or else you can do this without me."

"Okay, okay. Have it your way. All I'm saying is calm down."

"Drop it. Let's get on with this."

"You're lucky I've got no choice. You're a jerk," says Savannah, facing me with hands on hips.

I hear myself say, "Bug off, then." This isn't going how I planned.

Jack says, "Don't screw this up, Charlie," then turns to Savannah. "He's an idiot, but after he calms down he'll be sorry." He looks back at me and waits.

"Sorry, Savannah," I say.

She's still standing fiercely with her elbows out and feet planted. I put my hands out, palms up.

She sighs and drops her hands. "Okay, you big jerk."

"We need to move quickly and work together for safety," I say.

We split into pairs. Savannah and I take one side of the hall, Jack and Nolan the other. We start down the hall. Things seem normal, except for the sprawled body of the steward I hit with the sledge hammer. Looking down on him, I say, "We probably should move him."

"Won't somebody take care of him?" says Jack.

"From now on, we've got to get used to doing things for ourselves. We'll heave him overboard," I say.

We carry him to the nearest open deck and throw him overboard, then slowly work our way down the rest of the hall.

Nobody believes me. More than a few doors slam in my face. Savannah does better, so I let her do the talking. Most everyone takes the free food, and we quickly move on. Nolan and Jack have their routine down as they handle the other side of the hall, although most people seem to think it's a prank when told there's Ebola virus or the plague on board. We finish the tenth deck without any interruption from security. We get a few curious gazes as people pass by, but we do our best to look fierce, and no one stops us.

We move down to Deck 9 sometime around 8:30 p.m. Savannah looks thoughtful as we move along. She says, "There's two sections of cabins on each deck, one forward and one aft. Then there are fourteen rooms on each side of the hallway in each section, and a hallway on each side of the ship."

"That means one hundred and twelve rooms per deck," says Jack.

"Eight decks of passengers and another couple for the crew. How many people does that make?" she asks.

"Well, it's eleven hundred rooms," I say.

"Holy moly, how will we get to that many?" asks Nolan.

"Good thing we brought along the cart," says Jack.

Savannah looks at me. "There's no way we'll be able to get to them all."

"I don't think it's going to matter. I don't think it'll be safe farther down," I say.

We finish with the ninth and then the eighth deck around eleven o'clock. We've run out of food, but it's well past dinner time now anyway. After we abandon the cart, it goes faster. The decks are quiet, and we have no trouble. It's pretty late now, and a lot of people must be in bed already. Strange that no security officers have shown up.

As we move to the seventh deck, some of the people look scared at our news, instead of just annoyed. We can hear occasional shouts from below now. The danger escalates. We move urgently. A few people ask our advice about what to do. I suggest they wedge a desk chair under their door handle and nail the door closed if we don't get to land by the next night. I pull nails from my pocket for a few of them. They'll have to improvise and use a shoe or something as a hammer.

We take the elevator down to Deck 6, the lowest of the passenger decks. A gruesome sight confronts us when we turn into the corridor. The boys yelp in fear. A pile of bodies litters the floor a third of the way down the hall. Some of the cabin doors hang open, and the smell of blood is in the air. I motion urgently, finger to my lips to silence everyone.

We creep along the corridor and tap quietly on the first doors to the left and right. An eye blocks the peephole of the door before me, but it doesn't open.

"You need to barricade yourself in your room," I whisper to the eye.

"The ship isn't safe anymore," adds Savannah.

The door cracks open, and a sliver of whiskery face appears. "Huh?" says a gruff voice. We repeat ourselves.

"You think I don't know that, kid?" he says. "They"—he tilts his head toward the bodies down the hall—"already tried to warn us. Best get out of here and back to your parents *now*."

He's right. This is stupid. Anybody left alive on this deck is already on alert. They can see clearly what the dangers are as soon as they open their door.

"Let's go, guys," I say. I turn back toward the lobby, but it's already too late.

What's left of a man and woman, both still dressed in the ship's white uniforms, shuffle into the hall. The woman's head dangles half off her neck, and the man is missing an arm. We back away down the hall.

The man with the gruff voice takes a look at them and says, "Quick. Get out of here!" He steps out of his room and faces them, a dark handgun at the end of his stiff arms. How'd he get a gun on board ship with security so tight? He fires off two shots—*boom, boom*—both direct hits to the zombies' chests.

"Aim for the head!" I yell over the shouts of the boys.

But it's too late. They're on him as he fires again. This time the crewman's head explodes. The woman's head is harder to hit as it flops around. Unable to bite easily, she rips his flesh with both hands, fingernails digging into his face and down his neck. The man struggles all the way to the floor, the pistol firing wildly into the ceiling.

Savannah steps toward him, crowbar at the ready, but I grab her arm and pull her back. She sobs once and fights to pull her arm free.

"It's too late," I tell her, then more softly into her ear, "It's too late. Come on." Our protector lies bleeding out on the floor, the headless body of the woman lying on top of him. Her head rests nearby, teeth still chomping on empty air. Savannah's ragged breathing is loud in my ears as I pull her down the hall.

We scramble farther down the corridor and stumble over and around the other victims and their blood. I glance down and notice the empty holster at the dead officer's waist. Ah, the handgun. The corridor is long and enclosed, the end of it telescoping to appear impossibly far away. We run in panic. Jack and Nolan scream and skid to a stop in front of me. A zombie has entered the corridor from an open cabin ahead of us. Moaning comes from behind us. All the noise will bring more.

"Stupid, stupid, stupid!" a voice echoes in my head. How could I have led them down here without getting the shotguns first? Suddenly a zombie shoves a stateroom door open and makes a wild grab for me with its ragged fingers. It grabs me by the head and wrenches me closer. The boys scream. I remember what happened to Ben at death by chocolate. I whip my knife from my back pocket. The polished steel glints as I hold it with an overhand grip and ram it to the hilt into the zombie's temple. It drops like a stone. I pull out the knife and carefully wipe the blood off on the zombie's sleeve. I turn around and see Savannah and Nolan battering the other zombie with their crowbars.

Jack runs to the laundry room door. "In here!" he shouts, and pushes through the swinging door. We all tumble in behind him and scramble for an exit.

"Down here!" calls Nolan. He's already halfway into a laundry chute.

"No!" cries Savannah, gripping his leg with both hands. She hauls him out just in time. The laundry chute leads below to the crew area. There'd be no escape down there.

Jack leads the way to the door in the opposite wall and peeks through it. "All clear," he says.

We run for it. Zombies enter the laundry room as we leave. There are no bodies in this hall, and all the doors are tightly shut. We run full out for the end of the hall and take the stairs up two at a time.

We're on our way to our rooms when I remember I haven't gone after the shotguns yet. I hope it's not too late.

"I'm going after the guns. Jack, you come with me to help carry," I say.

"Okay," he replies, but no one wants to be left behind, so we all head up to the shooting area on Deck 12. It's deserted. I use the sledge hammer to break through the door and pry the lockbox open with my knife. My hands shake. Jack and I grab the four 20-gauge shotguns and sweep all the ammunition boxes from the lower shelf into a sack. I breathe a deep sigh of relief. We take the stairs back down to our room.

In front of us on the stairs, I meet the first zombie I'm actually prepared for. I bring the shotgun up, draw a bead on the monster's rotting head, and squeeze the trigger. *Click.* Crap! I forgot to load it!

I quickly tear open a box of ammo. The shells fly onto the floor as everyone screams. The zombie is only ten steps away but is having trouble getting up the stairs. I break the shotgun open and slide the bright yellow shell into the breech. The gun closes with a click, but the zombie is only five steps down now. It's close enough to fire from the hip, so I cock the hammer and cry, "Don't look!" I jerk the trigger.

Bang!

"Don't look," I tell everyone. "Trust me. You don't need to see another headless zombie." Gore splatters the carpeted stairway and walls.

We hurdle the bloody body, creep back to my parents' empty room on Deck 10, and slip silently inside. No one wants to be left alone after what we've gone through.

"Fill the sink with water, Jack. If the power goes out, we might not get any more."

"Why?" he says. He yawns so wide I can see the back of his throat. My eyes sting, and I feel that irresistible urge, too. It must be really late.

"Never mind. I'll do it," I tell him.

We push the beds together in one corner, shove the desk chair under the doorknob, and pile onto the bed. I look at Savannah. She's squeezed into the corner with her back against the wall, pillow hugged tight. Jack and Nolan burrow in next to her, leaving me on the outer edge of the bed, although the boys are tucked in so closely that there's empty space behind me. When I turn out the light, though, I feel the night spread out around us, full of menace. Someone's trembling shakes the bed. I'm too wired to sleep.

Despite the fearful tension straining all of us, there are still things that need to be said. I say quietly, "So far, guys, we haven't seen that much action."

"What do you mean, Charlie?" Nolan whispers. "That was a nightmare."

"It's going to get a whole lot worse tomorrow. Ten times worse, because that's how many more zombies there will be when we get up tomorrow." There's a stunned quiet after that.

"So, what do we do?" Savannah asks, her voice thin.

"When we get to Kiribati, the crew will be able to call for help. We'll get off the ship if we can or else sit tight right here and wait for rescue."

"Sounds good," Jack says.

But the future seems grim. I don't want to tell them just how bad. There will be dozens or hundreds of hungry undead tomorrow. We're trapped on a boat full of zombies.

Eventually everyone else goes to sleep. The bed is warm, and we're relaxed and cozy all piled together like this. I force myself to stay awake. There's work I need to do. I climb carefully from the bed and turn on the desk light to survey the room. We have plenty of supplies. When I've made a mental inventory, I take a notepad out onto the balcony, put my feet up, and start thinking. My head aches and my legs are twitchy. I'm exhausted, but I want to keep watch. I make a vow to be better prepared the next time they come at us. As I sit there, I envision what will happen next and plan for all possibilities. I make up a list of what we'll need to pack if we need to get to the island ourselves. The moon shines brightly, the night is warm, and the ocean glides by smoothly. With the ship silent, it's so peaceful that I can hardly believe anything is wrong.

Now and then in the night, though, the sound of voices crying out breaks the silence. One gurgling scream sounds close. I cringe every time, and can't help but imagine the horror happening outside our room. They must be thick down in the crew areas. The crew is clueless about what's going on. They don't have a chance. If any of them survive the night, they'll be attacked as soon as they leave their rooms in the morning.

Could I have prevented all of this if I'd taken Harry out two days ago instead of running away like a little kid? I wish Mom and Dad were here. Guilt and shame wash over me. A weight settles in my chest as my head drops, eyes squeezing closed in regret. Pressure builds in my chest, and I feel a hot pain behind my eyes as they fill with tears. None of it can be undone. I have a lot to make up for. I'll find a way to save us, I promise myself, as I look out at the night.

With new resolve, I pull out the big binder titled "Pacifica Ship's Guide" and start to read. There's a section for each of our ports of call. My stomach drops when I get to Kiribati, the next port. It's a small sliver of sand and palm trees, nothing more. The nearest real civilization, in Hawaii, is nine hundred miles away. The ship floats alone on the vast and empty expanse of the South Pacific.

Shifting in my seat and staring out at the night, I feel more and more uneasy. We should have reached land long before now. How many of the crew members are affected, either sick and dying or already reanimated? If there are not enough healthy crew members to pilot the ship to port, we could be out here drifting with the currents for weeks before help arrives. We have enough food and water for a while, but the zombies will hear us or smell us eventually. Despite our barricades, the door won't hold against them forever.

The sky lightens in the east when I spot an island in the distance. I rub my eyes to clear them, then squint again to be sure.

"Hey, guys, wake up, there's land in sight," I say as I rouse them. We all watch as the island grows larger. There's no visible civilization, but it's still far away. Something seems to be wrong, though. Instead of heading into the harbor, the ship looks like it's going to miss the island entirely. We're barely moving, and the ship seems to be listing a little to the port side. We come to a stop, but far from the island. Is the captain still in charge? Are we anchoring here, hundreds of yards offshore, or is the ship still drifting?

CHAPTER 19

DAY FIVE

Today we've got to get help. It's our only chance.

Under a clear sky, Kiribati looks like a movie paradise. From the tenth-floor deck, the island is laid out like a little jewel. It's a horseshoe-shaped sliver of land, an atoll with a long curve of beach embracing a lagoon. Farther inland a forest of coconut palms rises above the beach. The whole island looks like it is barely above high tide.

"Is that a building?" asks Nolan, hand shading his eyes. I grab binoculars for a closer look.

"Where?" I ask.

"In the middle of the island, just through the trees."

Looking through the binoculars again, I see it. A square metal roof. And sure enough, there's a satellite dish on top. We can only hope that there's a satellite phone connected to it. I don't think it's out here for watching TV.

We're too excited to sit as we wait for the announcement for disembarkation. But no announcement comes.

"I bet the ship's PA system got taken out by our firebomb," says Jack.

He's right. I haven't heard any announcements since then. I lift the handle on our phone. No dial tone. Stupid! Why didn't I think of that? Wouldn't Dad have been chewing me out on the phone for the last twelve hours if he could have?

We watch from the balcony to see whether anyone heads to the island. I remember the schematics of the ship from the Ship's Guide. There are small boats on the lower levels. Surely some of the crew will go ashore. The sun rises higher as we watch, but the ship is quiet. There's no sign of life. I begin to panic. What if there's no one in charge anymore? Isn't someone going to get us ashore before this horror show gets any worse?

I look back at the others and come to a decision. We'll have to go ourselves. We'll try the captain first, then get to the island ourselves if we have to. It'll be tough getting to the motor boats without help. They are far below, where the zombies are thickest. I contemplate jumping. The water doesn't look that far away, but it's about eight decks down to the water, almost a hundred feet. I'd be knocked unconscious. No, we'll have to go through the ship. We've got to get going and get into a boat.

After grabbing my lists, I start packing. "Load up your packs, guys. We need to get outta here. Everyone should have a supply of food, water, and weapons."

"What about the guns, Charlie?" asks Jack.

"We'll each take a gun."

"How do you fire it?" Savannah asks.

"Who's fired a gun before?" I say.

"I have. Pop taught me last summer, remember?" says Jack.

Nolan and Savannah are both silent. They look so young and innocent. This is nuts. I can't take them out there where the zombies roam. I'll have to get Dad and some of the other men.

"Okay, you guys stay in here. I'll go get Dad and Mom," I say.

They look at me with surprise.

"No way, Charlie. We want off the ship, too," says Jack. The other two nod.

I say, "We've done what we could. We warned a lot of people. We saved some lives yesterday. It's going to be a lot more dangerous today. I don't know that there's any crew left to run the ship, but our parents can take charge."

They protest, but I'm firm. I finish loading my pack, sling a shotgun over my back, and grab a crowbar. I pat my pocket and feel the shells there. "Stay put. I'll get Dad. He'll know what to do."

The time has come to leave the safety of our room. I check out the peephole before opening the door. Nothing. I crack the door open slowly and look out. Uh-oh. Zombies have been here. There's a body at the end of the hall by the stairs. I ease the door open and slide out.

"Good luck, Charlie," Savannah whispers.

I step quietly across to our room, where Mom and Dad are locked in.

"Dad," I call quietly. The doors are so soundproofed; I have to raise my voice before he can hear me.

"Charlie, you let us out of here immediately!" he shouts.

I slide the crowbar under the first nail. "I am, Dad. I was right. Zombies are taking over the ship. There's a body down the hall. Last night they were all over the lower decks."

His eye peers at me through the peephole. "What are you talking about?" he says.

"Zombies are taking over the ship."

The nail creaks loudly as I start to pull it out.

"Charlie, get us out of here. This has gone too far."

"I am, Dad. It's true. Jack and his friends took out a zombie in the communications room yesterday and trashed all the equipment. Haven't you noticed that your phone and TV don't work?" The nail comes free loudly, splintering the wood of the door. "I think the crew are all zombies. We're at Kiribati now, but we're at least twelve hours late, and I can't tell whether they even put an anchor down."

Savannah shouts behind me. "Charlie, <u>look out</u>! The noise is bringing them!"

I look around. A figure enters the corridor from the far end. Oh, no. I start on the second nail. I really drove them deep. This will take some time.

"Dad! They're coming! We need to get to land. There's a satellite dish, so maybe there's a way to communicate."

Jack steps into the hall as the second nail starts to give. He's got the shotgun to his shoulder, eye sighting down it and left foot a step ahead, just like Pop taught him.

"*Boom!*" the gun thunders. I look down the hall. He hit it, knocking it back some but missing the head. Only about thirty feet away now. Doors along the hallway crack open. The two ladies next door peer out, get an eyeful of armed kids and bodies scattered around, and slam the door shut again.

Jack struggles with his pack, digging for ammunition.

Mom and Dad shout inside the room now. The second nail gives way, and I pull it from the door. Only two to go. Jack reloads, and a second blast from the gun echoes in the hall as I start on the third nail.

"Look out! They're coming from both directions!" Savannah shouts behind me.

I turn and look. She's right. The one Jack shot lies still, but more come behind him and from the other side, too. Both ends of the hallway are thick with them, several of the clumsy figures bumping into one another in their hurry to get to us. We're making too much noise. Even more will be drawn to us. Savannah brings her crowbar to the ready as Nolan follows her into the hall.

"What's going on?" Dad shouts through the door.

I give his door a last wistful glance, then swing the shotgun around. I take aim and fire. Got one, but three more come behind it. I pull a shell from my pocket and break the gun open to load.

"Dad, there's too many!" I yell.

I look up and down the hall, trying to think of who might help. Mr. Schaefer in 1016 uses a walker. Next door to them is a younger guy, who's forty-something, I think. I pound on his door. "We need some help out here!" I shout.

"Get lost, kid!" he yells.

I look around, thoughts racing, and pound on other doors, but no one answers. It's chaos in the hallway, but only two zombies are left in one direction.

"I'm going! Cover me, Jack," I yell and run down the hall towards them.

"We're coming with you!" shouts Savannah, and their footsteps sound behind me. I pause to aim and fire— *boom!*—

and the zombie pitches onto its face. As I run I grab another shell and break the shotgun open. When I slow down to reload, the other kids catch up with me. I drop another zombie. Now the path is clear to the end of the hall.

I risk a glance behind me, the staggering undead mob the narrow hall. The leader stumbles and falls like a bag of bones, and the others walk right over him. They're not fast, so we easily outrun them. If the other zombies cut us off, though, we're dead.

We hurry down the rest of the hall onto the landing, eyes swiveling as we enter. All clear. I press the "up" button on the elevator and watch the lights as I wait for it. The others' backs are to me as they watch the halls. When the shuffling monsters enter the lobby, we huddle at the elevator door. "*Bing!* announces its arrival, and I swivel to take aim at the doors. They slide open to an empty elevator. We pile in, and I push the button for Deck 12, doors closing just before the reach of gruesome fingers can stop them.

I look around at the others. Their eyes are wild, but they've all got their backpack on and have weapons in hand. Jack's baseball bat sticks up from his pack. As we rise, I help Nolan and Savannah to sling the shotguns over their shoulders and then readjust their packs. Jack and I reload.

The elevator doors open to an empty deck. We creep quietly down the hall to the bow of the ship and start up the stairs. I hope that by keeping to the higher decks we will avoid trouble for as long as possible. We'll try one more time to get help—if that fails we're completely on our own.

"We're going to the captain," I say.

I lead them to the narrow stairs that end in the lobby behind the bridge. We creep silently up the carpeted steps to the top. It's completely silent as my head comes level with the lobby floor, the others close behind me.

Oh, no. Fresh blood flows from the neck of a uniformed officer lying in front of the door to the bridge. He's been attacked, and recently, I think, by the undead lying around him. Two other officers with the gray and mottled skin of reanimation lie next to him, bullet wounds in their head. I tiptoe to the window in the bridge. Maybe it's not too late to get help from the bridge. I step around the bodies and look through the window. A hand seizes my ankle. I gasp, jump back, and whip the shotgun around.

"You've got to get help," the injured officer says in a weak whisper.

I kneel beside him as the others join me. I recognize him as the big security officer from my earlier visit to the bridge.

"The Captain's sick," he says. The keening coming through the doors to the bridge confirms it's worse than that.

After rummaging through her pack, Savannah pulls out the first aid kit and brings it to me. "I don't know what to do," she says, looking desperately at the array of Band-Aids, gauze, and antibiotic ointment.

"Nothing can help him now, Savannah."

"Are there any other passengers left alive?" the dying man asks me.

"Oh yeah. I think most of the passengers are locked in their cabins," I reply.

"Sully organized a group to warn the passengers deck by deck. Did he make it?"

I grimace. "Don't think so."

The officer clutches my shirt. "You've got to go for help. There's a satellite phone and a generator on the island."

"What about the rest of the crew?" I ask.

"Everyone's lost. There may be some crew members barricaded in their cabins, but all the officers are dead or worse." He shivers as he speaks.

"What happened?" asks Jack as he and Nolan gather around.

The officer speaks haltingly, "Two days ago there were injuries. Everybody . . . sick in bed. The next day, they went nuts and started biting everyone." He catches his breath, panting a little. "Attacked their bunkmates, then anyone in the halls. By the time we caught them, dozens more dead or injured . . ." He stops.

Nolan pats his arm.

The officer continues yet more slowly, "It snowballed. Last night the decks were a death zone. Came up here to guard the bridge, but the captain had already been infected. We've . . . hold onto the bridge and got to port . . . no navigator or pilot. I went . . . check on communications and . . . chased me back up." He draws a shuddering breath. "Anybody alive on the bridge?"

Jack looks through the window. "The captain's the only one moving, but he's not alive anymore," says Jack.

"We tied the captain up when we figured out what was going on, but he must have got loose," the officer says weakly. "Go to Kiribati and call help. Get here in a day."

"Okay, but what about you? What can we do?" Savannah says.

"Get these kids out of here," he says and looks at me. "Then . . . what you need to do. Don't want to end up like them."

I know what he's telling me to do. I glance at his name badge and say, "Don't worry. I'll take care of you, Seamus. Boys, spread out and keep a lookout."

"We'll stay with you," Savannah says to the dying seaman. She sits next to him and takes his hand.

He looks at her. "Are they zombies, like in movies?"

"Yeah," she says and looks at me.

"It's a textbook zombie infection," I say. "It started with the magician, but I don't know how he got infected."

"Before he died, Harry said . . . got cursed in del Diablo," Seamus says, his voice barely audible. His eyes close.

"Stay with us," says Savannah, squeezing his hand.

He opens his eyes, looks into hers, and says, "I wish I could have done more."

"You did enough. We can take it from here," she replies. A tear tracks down her cheek.

"We'll get to the island," I say.

His eyes flicker up to mine, and I think I see him nod, and then he's still.

"Seamus! Seamus!" says Savannah, nudging his shoulder.

I watch for his chest to rise again and put my face close to feel his breath. "I think he's dead," I say.

Savannah's distressed and tear-filled eyes meet mine. I feel sick to my stomach about what comes next.

"Take the boys and go down to twelve and wait for me," I say. I take his sidearm, and stand, wiping my hand on my pants as they leave. A gun would be too loud. The M9 is heavy in my hand. We can't afford to attract any more attention if we're going to get out of here. My stomach heaves as I contemplate this, but finally I tuck the gun in my waistband and take the sledge hammer from my pack, close my eyes, and do what I must for him. I turn and throw up in the corner, then wipe my mouth and hurry down the stairs.

The faster we can get to that satellite phone, the faster we'll all be saved. I'm thinking hard as I catch up to the others on the pool deck. I've got a plan, and I start explaining it quietly. We're all nervous, but I talk them through it.

"There's a set of external ladders from the rear deck by the pools that leads down to level three. The ladders end only feet away from the nearest launch," I begin. "We just take the ladder down and then lower a boat into the water and ride to Kiribati."

It looked simple on the map last night. There's one problem, though. My brother.

"Jack, you're not going to be able to do this. It's too high. We'll take you back to the cabin first."

"You're not leaving me behind. I want off this ship, too."

"It's more than a hundred feet down to the water. There's no way."

"You can't stop me. If you take me to the room, I'll just follow you back up here."

I rub my forehead. How do I deal with this?

Jack stands stubbornly in front of me.

I look at the others. They stand behind Jack, looking at me.

"Okay," I tell him. "But if you can't do it, you'll have to make it back to our room alone."

"I can do it," he says.

We reach the stern, the sun shining brightly down on the clean decks and pools, the ocean smooth and sparkling on all sides. We're bunched together, each of us carrying a backpack filled with supplies. We each have a shotgun slung over our back, and everyone carries a hammer or crowbar.

For a moment, I wonder how on earth it got this bad. From here, the ship looks the same as it ever did. The sunshine is bright and the pools look inviting. We walk quietly to the stern near the surf pool. I locate the stairs, which are shallow metal emergency steps that drop almost to water level. It's a dizzying view from the top, and I feel a touch of vertigo. I hadn't expected that it was quite that far.

Nolan sticks his head over the railing and looks down the ladder. He whistles softly. "That's a heck of a long drop."

"Uh, Charlie, I think we could take the elevator down. That'd be a lot simpler," says Jack.

"Not a chance. Too many zombies. Should we take you back to the room now?"

He shakes his head stubbornly.

"Okay, then." I tighten the straps on my pack and swing a leg over the side. I grip the rail and start down. "Stay close behind me," I say before I continue.

I count the rungs as I go. Thirty-nine rungs and I'm level with Deck 11. Above me Nolan and then Savannah climb on the ladder. Another thirty-nine rungs and I'm down to Deck 10. So far, so good. I look up. Jack leans over the railing, still standing on the deck. Uh-oh. Should I go back up for him? There's no way he'll be able to climb down this far.

He shouts, then disappears from view. I'm frozen, eyes focused upward, hoping to see him reappear. How could I leave him up there?

"Jack!" calls Nolan.

A body tumbles over the railing, nearly hitting Savannah on its way down, and splashes into the water. In panic, I look down to the water to see if it was him that fell. A woman's arm sinks slowly into the water. That's a relief. My hands tighten on the rungs, eyes straining up past Nolan and Savannah, hoping he's still there. He's not. I scramble up, struggling to pass Nolan and find my brother.

His head pops over the rail.

"Jack, are you all right?" I call.

"Yeah."

"Hold on. I'm coming." The boat will have to wait.

"Had to take one out." He holds up his baseball bat, the end dark with blood. "I'm going to do this." Surprisingly, he swings his leg over the rail and grabs the ladder. For a moment he freezes.

"You can do it. It's just a ladder," I call softly. He nods and swings his other leg over. I exhale and start back down.

"How far is it?" Jack says. He cranes his neck to the side to look down.

"Don't look down!" I say harshly, then I lie, "Only a couple more decks to go, and then we're home free."

After a half dozen decks, the ladder seems endless. One glance through the window of Deck 5, though, is enough to keep me hustling. Brain-dead figures wander the crew lounge, occasionally bumping into the walls. Their senseless murmurs penetrate the glass. I hurry down, but not before one sees me. It heads straight for me, arms outstretched, and slams into the window.

"Faster!" I call to the others, climbing lower.

The banging on the window above gets louder.

Nolan stops and stares when he reaches the window. Figures crowd in front of him, flinging themselves at the glass. Savannah nudges him on with her toes, then cringes as she comes even with the window. The glass cracks loudly in front of her. Savannah jumps and shrieks. They're breaking through!

We scramble down as fast as we can. Luckily, the hull is solid on the next level down.

Finally, I reach level three, where the launches are. There's a strip of deck against the hull of the ship that widens as it heads forward to the boat. It's just wide enough to grip with my toes, but most of my size thirteen Nikes dangle above open ocean. I shuffle toward the boat and finally stand solidly on the deck. The motorboat rests only three feet away. Unfortunately, zombies stand on the deck, facing away for now, but they can't help but see me soon.

After Nolan and Savannah reach the deck, breaking glass sounds from above. I look up. The zombies above us on the fifth deck have broken all the way through the window. Many arms reach through the hole, but I don't think they can climb down the ladder. The first ones to come out only plunge into the ocean. Luckily, they miss Jack on the way down. The splashing attracts the zombies on my deck. They tumble over the railing and crash into the ocean, too, drawing the attention of even more zombies. Fortunately, the boat is out of their reach.

I pat my brother on the back as he climbs into the boat. "Good job, bro."

While the others load the packs into the boat, I work out how the winch works. I lower them slowly down the ten feet or so to the ocean below. I pull off my shoes, toss them down to the boat, then throw Jack the line.

"Watch out for zombies, Charlie!" Jack yells as I jump into the water.

The ocean looked so calm from the ship, but once I'm in the water the swells rise frighteningly high above me. With each one I'm tossed dangerously between ship and launch. Little by little, I fight my way to the others and lever myself into the boat.

I say, "They can't swim. They sink when their lungs fill with water."

"Cool," says Nolan.

"Yeah, but they can walk around on the ocean floor until they find land," I say.

"Ew, wish I didn't know that," says Savannah.

CHAPTER 20

Piloting the launch is a piece of cake. All the controls are clearly marked, and the engine starts easily. We motor to the island a couple hundred yards away, and pull the boat onto the sand. The sun is high—must be getting close to lunch time. The peaceful beach, palm trees, and blue sky surround us.

The island is probably no more than twenty acres, a narrow strip of land only a few feet above high tide. A forest of palm and other trees with heavy scrub extends to the edge of the beach. A sandy path leads to a small metal shed on the highest part of the island. As we approach the shed, the satellite dish on the roof is clearly visible, along with a generator that sits under the flat roof. A golf cart is plugged into the generator. Stacks of beach chairs and umbrellas lean against the building. There's a padlock on the door, but I strike the lock twice with the sledge hammer, and the door springs open. Light filtering through a torn curtain reveals a desk covered with canvas that dominates the room.

Nolan pulls the cloth off the desk, scattering dust through the air. "Hey, a phone!" He lifts the receiver. "It's dead."

"We need to get the generator going," I say. I leave Nolan and Jack at the desk, pulling papers out of the desk drawer. Savannah follows me outside to the generator. The shade on the porch is not much cooler than it was under the hot sun. I squat for a closer look. The generator looks simple enough to use. There's a fuel valve and a power switch. I turn both on. Nothing happens.

Maybe it's out of gas. I find the fuel tank and tap it. Empty. I dig around and find some diesel nearby in a cupboard under the porch roof. I pour it into the generator using a funnel from the cupboard. The fuel doesn't look right, though. It's too dark, and it has chunks of stuff in it. I try the power switch again, and this time it starts with a loud, chugging sound. Jack sticks his head out of the shack and cheers. Black smoke pours from the engine, and it coughs to a stop.

"It may not have run for a long time," says Savannah.

"Mmm."

Now what? I look for the instruction manual in the shed, but don't find it. I kneel in the sand and start looking the generator over, searching for the problem. I check the oil level and add some. I start it up again, but it still belches dark smoke. It's running rough, too. This can't be good. I flip the switch off.

Jack pops out again. "Charlie, turn that back on. We need to get the phone working."

"It's not running right. Give me a minute."

He groans and goes back in.

I sit on the sand and examine all the parts, thinking hard. The shade edges away, leaving me in the hot sun. I'm sweaty and tired.

Jack comes out and says, "Why don't we turn it on?"

"Bug off."

"All right, all right," he says, holding his hands defensively in front of him, and goes back in.

Maybe the fuel is too old. It doesn't look right. Luckily, I remember the launch holds several cans of diesel. I return to the boat and open the diesel carboy. Yep. The fuel looks clearer and lighter than what I put in the generator. I haul the big tank across the island, wiping sweat from my face with a mostly clean arm. I wish I could use the golf cart for this, but it isn't charged.

I top off the tank and start it up again. More smoke. When I'm done coughing, I kick the stupid thing. Maybe if I drain the old fuel and refill the tank. Two screws hold the fuel tank in place, but we have screwdrivers in the packs. I look up for the first time in a while. No one's around. Where are they?

I find them behind the shed, goofing off. Jack's pack sits open on the ground, spilling food. He's back in the trees throwing rocks in the air. Nolan lies under a palm reading.

I gather up the food and call, "Jack, you idiot, look at the bugs in our food!"

"That's my pack," says Nolan.

"Uh, sorry. Can't you guys keep focused for just one afternoon? I'm working my butt off to get the generator going, and you're all off playing Swiss Family Robinson."

"Chill out, Charlie, we're working," says Savannah, coming out from the trees with an armload of branches.

"Yeah, Jack's working hard at throwing rocks at trees, I can see that."

I grab a screwdriver from the ground and stomp back to the generator. My head pounds, and black specks dance in front of my eyes. I need some sleep. I feel the others gathering around me, watching. Eventually I fumble the screws off and dump the fuel tank, rinse it with the good diesel and refill it. After I flip both switches on, the generator chugs to life and runs smoothly. I stare stupidly at it. I actually fixed it.

"Woo-hoo!" Jack and Nolan jump into the air and chest-bump.

When I get to my feet, my head spins. Savannah grabs my arm.

"Charlie, you need to take a break."

"Huh?"

"When was the last time you slept?"

"Night before last, I guess.

"When was the last time you ate?"

"Don't remember. Listen, I don't have time for this. I need to get the phone working."

"Nolan's been studying the instructions all afternoon. He's going to do the phone," she says. "You need to rest."

"Huh?" I press my hand to my forehead. Feels like a vise is clamped over my temples. My head throbs. "I've got a bitch of a headache." I can't think straight.

"I got this," Nolan says.

"Come on, Charlie. There's some Tylenol in the first aid kit." She leads me away and hands me some pills and a water bottle.

"Wouldn't hurt you to clean up, too. You stink."

I look down. My hands are black with grease, and my pants are smeared with grease and dried blood. I reek. I look up and try to clear my eyes. Savannah looks fresh and clean.

"Maybe I could take a short break." She hands me a travel size bottle of shampoo and walks away.

I look around. Palm trees block the view of the ship and harbor. In the other direction, the empty ocean stretches to the horizon. We're safe enough here now, but it's dangerously exposed if something goes wrong.

I grab my pack and wander down the beach to an isolated spot. The water is warm. I scrub down. I scrounge a fresh T-shirt and shorts from my pack, and a slender nail falls out with them. I wander farther down the beach to find a shady spot to sit. I worry the nail into a curve as I walk until it looks like a hook. I unclasp my paracord bracelet and use a pocket knife to cut the cord loose. Once I unwind all seven feet of cord, I tease the fibers from its interior and pull them out one end. By tying the seven strands end-to-end, I've got almost 50 feet of line that I knot onto my hook. I dig out a sand crab from under its air hole on the beach and spear it with the hook. I munch an apple as I cast out and sit in the shade of a palm to wait. The sun is hot, and the sand is warm. My eyelids are heavy . . .

I wake with a start. The line jerks over my hand where I've got it threaded through my fingers. I stand and reel it in. An elegant fish, heavy and almost two feet long thrashes at the end. The body is a milky white, but the fins and tail are sharply pointed and dark.

My stomach rumbles. The sun is low in the sky. Must be getting to dinnertime. I clean the fish, and wash it in the ocean before making my way back to the others.

Savannah has set up camp on the beach near the shed. They've placed rocks in a circle for a fire pit. Jack adds branches to a pile of firewood at the edge of the beach. I arrange some dried palm fronds in the pit and lay branches over them, then pull a lighter from my pack. I soon nurse the flame into a blaze. Jack and Nolan sit next to me on logs around the fire.

Savannah lays out some fruit.

"How'd you get the coconuts?" I ask.

"Jack knocked them out of the trees with a rock," she replies.

"Guess those bazillion hours playing baseball were good for something," I say.

Jack smiles.

"Nolan, did you get the phone to work?" I ask.

"Yeah, it works," he says.

"Did you call for help?" I ask.

"Yeah, I did," he says. "It was a lot of work. I had to figure out how to turn the satellite dish, then I had to figure out the country codes. "

"Who'd you call?" I ask.

"I'm hungry. Let's talk about it later," he says.

Evasive.

"We'll try again tomorrow," Savannah says.

I roast the fish over the fire, and everyone gathers around. Jack and Nolan crack the coconuts open with a hammer. As the sun falls into the sea, we dig in and gorge ourselves on fish, fruit, and coconut milk.

After dinner, I wash my hands in the ocean, then lay the guns out on the mat.

"You think we're going to need these now?" asks Savannah. "Isn't help on the way?"

We all look at Nolan.

He shrugs sheepishly. "I hope so. Seems good to be prepared no matter what."

I grab one of the shotguns. "This is a single-barrel, break-action shotgun. It breaks open, and you put the shell in, close it, and then you just have to pull the trigger." I demonstrate. "Now you guys try."

In the light of a flashlight, everyone mimics loading, then aims and fires the empty shotguns. I practice with the M9 semiautomatic before sticking it into my waistband. With just a sliver of moon, it's dark as a cave by the time we lay blankets out around the dying fire and stretch out on them.

"Everyone needs some sleep. I'll keep watch for a while," I say.

I stay up late making plans and getting the camp organized. After storing all our gear in the packs, I look around. What am I missing? I look out at the ocean and then into the trees. It doesn't feel secure. I dig through the trash left inside the building until I find a dozen soda cans. I improvise some noisemakers at the periphery of our camp by half-filling the cans with pebbles and balancing them on rocks. Most of these I put on the footpath or on the beach, since the underbrush makes movement through the palm forest difficult.

I still don't feel secure. It's too unprotected here.

I enter the shed and shake my head. There's no way to blockade the window. I look up. The roof might do. I grab my full pack, climb on top of the golf cart, then pull myself up onto the shed roof. I'm now higher than the zombies can reach. But if I can climb up that easily, a zombie could do it, too. I start up the freshly-charged cart and drive it away from the building, then lean some lawn chairs against the side of the shed. It's harder now to reach the roof, but still possible by stepping onto the folded chairs. With my feet planted on the roof, I stare into the darkness. In daylight, the view will be clear across the island to the ship. I leave the backpack on the roof and climb down.

When the moon has slipped lower in the sky and it's well past midnight, I wake Jack for the next watch and go to sleep.

CHAPTER 21

When I wake, I'm already on my feet, toes dug deep in the sand and gun in hand.

I hear Jack's urgent whisper, "Charlie, I heard something."

It's pitch black. I can't see him or anything else. The fire has died down so that not even the coals glow. The moon must have set or been covered by a cloud. I can't see Jack but he sounds like he's somewhere to my left. The fire pit must be to my left, as well, and the waves lap the beach to my right. A rustling comes from somewhere beyond Jack, which means it's probably beyond the camp in the trees.

"Did anybody leave camp? Did you notice?" I ask as I step toward him gingerly, avoiding the fire pit.

"I could hear everyone breathing. We're all still here."

I scan what must be the trees, but all is blackness. There, I hear it again. It's my homemade alarm, the sound of pebbles rattling in a can. A quiet shuffling follows. It's hard to tell in the dark, but it sounds as if someone's maybe thirty feet away.

"Do you have a light?" I whisper.

"I've got some matches in my pocket.

I grab his arm and gesture toward the trees. "Light a match and throw it toward the trees."

A match flares, then flies dying into the darkness. It doesn't go far or shed much light, but unfortunately it doesn't have to. The brief flash reveals a shambling figure approaching us along the path, now only fifteen feet away.

I step forward to meet it and blindly squeeze the trigger of the semiautomatic. *Boom, boom, boom!* The reports deafen me and wake everyone.

Another flash of light reveals that it's still coming. *Crap!*

I fire quickly, my hands shaking. The next shot hits it in the middle of the chest. The impact knocks the zombie backward but doesn't stop it. As I reload, the stink of rotting flesh sickens me and I feel an inhuman chill. I'm panting now from the adrenaline rush. At the last second, I blast its head off at point-blank range.

Someone's found a flashlight, which scans the woods. I squint into the darkness beyond our camp, my eyes following the beam of light. I strain to hear movement.

"There!" Nolan shouts, pointing. "I see one!"

I fire. Got him! But there are others beyond it, attracted by our shouts and the gunfire.

There're too many! *We're overrun!*

I shout, "Run to the building. Climb on top!"

Savannah grabs her shotgun as the boys run for it.

"Behind you!" she shouts, aiming her gun.

I spin. A zombie slogs out of the surf. It lurches, dripping, onto the beach. I back away and reload quickly.

I pull the trigger. *Got him!*

I turn and dash for the hut. In two steps, I vault over the chairs and jump for the roof. I pull myself up, bare toes scrabbling on the metal wall. An icy hand grasps my ankle. Savannah stands on the rooftop, gun at her hip. She fires past me. *Boom!* My ears ring. A cold sludge sprays my bare legs. I jerk my leg free and scramble onto the roof. Breathing hard, I stand on the rooftop and look down.

Oh, God!

"They're coming!" Savannah screams.

I lean over the edge of the roof, my friends' hands holding me in place, and use the barrel of a shotgun to knock the lounge chairs away from the wall.

Hungry groans come from below. We scramble to the middle of the roof. At only ten feet from the ground, we're barely out of their reach.

The zombies scratch at the walls. Eerie sounds wash over us. They climb over one another in their frenzy to have us. Savannah continues to load and fire.

"Hold your fire," I tell her. "We can't kill them all, and we're wasting ammunition firing into the dark."

We stand with our guns at the ready, breathing hard.

"Everybody okay?" I ask, looking at the boys. They are small and shivering in the shaky beam of the flashlight.

CHAPTER 22

DAY SIX

As the sun rises over the trees, I take a mental inventory.

We're on a ten-by-twelve-foot island of safety in a sea of zombies. This is so worse than being on the ship. They claw at the walls below us. They have broken down the door and shattered the window.

The four of us sit cross-legged on the roof with the supplies between us, our heads nodding from lack of sleep.

The shed shivers underneath us.

We have three shotguns, with some ammo still in my pockets, the M9, plus my sledge hammer, the screwdriver, and a crowbar, and each of us has a knife in our belt. There's enough food to last us only a day or so. Savannah's pack holds the first aid kit, another flashlight, and some shotgun shells.

Jack's got his precious baseball bat, which he probably sleeps with even back home. He's the only one wearing shoes.

We don't seem anything like the army we'd felt ourselves to be a day ago.

Savannah passes out crackers and cheese while we talk things over. The wheezing sighs of the undead are loud around us, but that's not what takes away my appetite. I could ignore that if I had to, but I'm sickened by the wet scraping sounds their bodies make as they pull barehanded at the shed.

"Nolan, is help coming?" asks Jack.

His head down, he says, "I'm not sure."

"What do you mean, you're not sure?" I ask sharply. "Our lives depend on it."

Savannah says, "Who did you reach? Did they say they'd be here soon?"

"Well, I tried calling 911, but it didn't ring through."

"That's only in the U.S.," I say, my voice carrying a note of discouragement.

" Don't worry," says Savannah. "Who else?"

"I finally got a hold of an international operator who connected me with the L.A. police department. They didn't believe me at first, but I think I convinced the dispatcher that I was serious."

"That's good. The police will know what to do," adds Jack.

Nolan frowns. "Sorry guys, I thought I'd have more time. I was gonna look through the manuals in there and find the right emergency numbers, but then I lost the satellite connection."

Holding my feelings in, shoulders tense, I look away from the group. Off in the distance, the ship shimmers on the ocean.

The sun heats up the metal roof under us. We're baking, and we have no way to get down to our water supply. Seamus said that rescuers could get to us in twenty-four hours. I squint at the sun again and make a calculation. Must be about twelve hours since Nolan's calls. We won't last another night up here.

On the wall below us, the cables running to the satellite dish are completely shredded. No more phone calls from here. I need to come up with a different plan.

The shed shakes even more violently. I brace myself on hands and knees, nudging the boys to the center. The porch roof over the generator shudders. A crack appears between it and the main roof. Savannah screams.

With a tremendous noise, the porch roof starts to break away. They've taken out the posts that supported it. With one corner of the porch still attached to the main roof and the other end on the ground, there's a ramp from the ground to us. A figure shambles onto the end and tilts its way upward. More follow.

Jack shoots down at them, the gun's report echoing over Savannah's screams.

Kneeling, I swing the sledge hammer and slam it down on the porch roof just beyond the crack. The shed shudders.

Will the whole thing come down? I have to chance it. I have no other options. I swing the sledge hammer again, this time pounding the exposed bolts holding the porch to the shed. Arms straining, I put all my weight into it. The crack widens. I swing harder. The other three yell.

I swing again and again. The porch gives way and crashes to the ground, taking the zombies with it. The shed rocks wildly. Zombies strain to reach us, but we're safe for the moment. Won't be long, though, before they pull the whole building down.

I feel close to despair. No time now to wait for rescue. None of us will be alive by the time it comes.

I close my eyes and struggle to think. My brother grabs my hand. What can we do.?

Savannah says, "We knew we wouldn't stay here forever. Nolan did what he could with the sat phone."

Nolan hangs his head.

"It wouldn't matter who you called, Nolan. Nobody could get to us this quick," says Jack.

I look around. Zombies hobble aimlessly among the palm trees. Several launches rock in the surf. Other passengers must have had the same idea of escaping to the island, but they brought the plague with them.

"No matter how bad the ship is, we're better off there. It's certain death if we stay here," says Savannah. She looks intently at each of us.

"We're going back to the ship," she says.

CHAPTER 23

"We've got to go back to the ship. We can take the golf cart as far as the beach," she says again.

I nod. If we go quickly enough, we might make it. I shoulder the largest pack.

"Are you sure?" Jack looks doubtfully around the shed.

"We can't stay up here forever. It'll be worse when those bodies on the beach zombify," Savannah says. She's already swinging down to the ground to stand unsteadily on the pile of bodies. She leans one arm on the shed and reaches up for the pack. A gray-skinned man lurches for her. I scramble for the shotgun. I fire and take the zombie down. Nolan jumps nimbly down and lands with bent legs on the pile.

Boom! I clear out another of the undead from their path.

Jack sits on the edge of the roof. I pull out the M9 and fire two rounds at zombies staggering towards Savannah and Nolan. More are coming, almost on them now! Jack rolls onto his stomach at the roof's edge, and pauses to look down.

"Jack, you've got to move!" I shift position for a better line and fire again. He dangles with legs swinging over the drop.

"Come on, bro!" I bump Jack on the shoulder with my foot. He drops awkwardly, hitting the ground hard and falling backward into Nolan.

I fire again, then drop down and scramble for the cart.

Nolan and Savannah are already inside, with guns swiveling wildly. Jack jumps on the back as I slide in next to Savannah.

She cranks the key to ON, and floors the gas pedal. The golf cart rumbles to life, but too slowly. I know that every zombie on the island is on its way here.

We bounce along the path to the beach. Ahead and behind, the undead close in on us. We veer from side to side to avoid them, but one of them snags Savannah's arm. It almost pulls her off the cart until she grabs onto me and I yank her back in.

"Hold on!" She crashes into the next one, *ca-chunk*, and then the next. The impact jars the cart so much at this speed that the wheels briefly leave the ground. I brace myself against the frame of the cart.

She swerves left and right, avoiding some of them, plowing down others. If I make it out of here, the game of golf will never be the same again.

We roll onto the beach, and the golf cart quickly bogs down in the sand. We've got a lead on them, though.

Our launch is still beached where we left it, water lapping at its sides. It's a beautiful scene except for the bodies that litter the shore.

We run for the boat. The other three climb in, and I push the boat into the surf and scramble on board.

The engine catches quickly, and I steer the boat into the glassy water of the lagoon.

We take one last look at Kiribati from the shelter of the lagoon, then turn to the work ahead— all of us except Savannah, who frowns severely at the tip of the island as we pass, one hand shading her eyes.

I turn to reassure her, but she's gone. Before I can react, she dives over the side and swims hard for the shore.

"Savannah, are you nuts?" I shout at her, knowing that she can't hear me. As she pulls for the island, a small movement catches my eye. A toddler stumbles down to the water, arms flailing, mouth open in a scream.

Oh, no, she's going back for him. She's a short swim from the beach, but already the undead are coming, drawn by the baby's wailing. Adrenaline surges through me.

I swing the boat around and head back, but already it's too late. The little kid turns and reaches out to a shambling figure steadily closing the distance between them.

Savannah reaches the bigger waves now that slam into the island's unprotected outer coast. She looks back just as a huge wave slams over her and catapults her toward the shore. The dead thing reaches out for the boy. Savannah plunges through the surf toward the child, who's only yards away.

Other shapes emerge from the forest and lurch toward the noise. Savannah's arms pump as she splashes to the child and snatches him up, right from under the greedy fingers of another zombie.

I'm still a hundred feet from shore, but am closing in fast. "Run, Savannah," I whisper.

With the child in one arm, Savannah heads down the beach. More and more of the walking dead are drawn by the commotion. They converge on Savannah. Some are almost close enough to touch, but she threads her way through the pack like a

119

running back. She breaks into a flat-out sprint. Boy, can she run. She pulls away from the monsters on the beach, giving me an opening where I can meet them with the boat.

I throttle back as I near the beach. Jack and Nolan pull Savannah and the wailing child onboard. I slam the engine into reverse, turn, and plow into the waves.

The boys cheer.

Zombies shuffle straight into the surf and keep going.

Savannah looks at me. "You're a total nut," I shout to her over the engine noise.

"I know," she replies with a smile.

As we near the ship, I cut the engine. Best to creep up quietly on them. The child is slumped in Savannah's arms, whimpering softly. He must be worn out from crying so hard.

"Jack and Nolan, grab a paddle. We're going to row."

I take up a paddle from my position towards the front, too. The ocean tosses us, but steady paddling gradually brings us around to the stern of the ship.

"What are we going to do with him?" Nolan asks.

"Our parents should still be in their rooms. We'll give him to them for now," I reply.

"You mean I just show up after being out all night? What are they gonna think? My dad is gonna kill me. Or he'll kill you," says Savannah.

"You may be surprised. They could have changed their tune by now."

"You better stay out of his sight anyway," says Nolan.

The ship looms overhead, more silent than when we left. Vague shapes wander the open decks. They're most dense on the lower levels. We tie off to the ladder. The boys silently climb on board, and start up the ladder.

Savannah gazes back at the island wistfully. "It was like such a paradise—in the beginning."

"There are other islands out there," I say. "Right now we've got another problem." I gesture at the now sleeping toddler then at the ship above us. "How do we get him up that ladder?"

She looks at him and twists her mouth in concentration.

I swing a loop of rope around the little guy's waist.

"You can't do that!" says Savannah.

"What do you mean? What else can I do?"

"You'll have to carry him up," she says.

Releasing the rope, I lift him by the armpits. Heavy. I slide him under one arm at my hip and reach the other hand up to grab a rung of the ladder above me. He stirs and starts to cry. I shake my head. Too heavy. Too loud, too, if he cries the whole way.

I empty out my backpack and cram him in. He squeals and reaches for Savannah. I can't close the pack even when I push down on his head.

"Charlie, Stop!" Savannah says, and pulls him back into her lap to quiet him. As soon as he's back snug in her arms, his head droops and eyelids close.

I run my hands through my hair.

OK, I got this. Grabbing up the backpack again, I pull out my knife and cut two holes in the bottom.

I hold up the open pack. "Slip him in."

With Savannah holding him tight to her, we gently wiggle his legs through the holes and ease the pack up his torso. I slowly zip the top closed over his head. He never wakes.

I slide one arm through a strap. Savannah shifts his weight onto my back and loops the other strap over my shoulder.

I start up the ladder, moving slowly so I don't wake my passenger. Savannah follows. Jack and Nolan are already out of sight on the top deck.

It's a long and difficult climb with the baby's weight pulling me backward. When we finally reach the top, the boys are gone.

Savannah says, "Where'd they go?"

I shrug. "They have the shotguns and know how to use them," I say, but I'm worried, too.

The deck is clear, so we creep across it to the stairs midship, senses on high alert, and start down to Savannah's parents' room.

As we round the curve in the stairs, I freeze. My heart's racing and sweat runs down my back. What's wrong? I stand silently on the stairs. At the edge of my hearing is an oh-so-faint but familiar sound. A low moan, almost animal-like. I grab Savannah's arm and lead her back the way we came and out the swinging door to the deck. Keeping her behind me, I put my eye to the crack between door and frame. After a few seconds, a pair of lady zombies in swimsuits—ugh, that's gonna haunt me for a lifetime—stumble up the stairs and out of sight.

Once they're gone, we sneak down the stairs. I whisper to Savannah, "If we're careful, maybe we can avoid them. If we hear them moaning, we'll just get out of their way."

"They're not very smart," she says.

"Lucky for us."

The toddler starts to cry in my backpack. Savannah unzips the top. The boy reaches out for her, his face flushed and his eyes red.

"Come here. Don't cry, little guy," she says, wiping his tears away.

"Try to keep him quiet," I say.

She bounces him on her hip until he stops crying.

I lead the way again, and in silence we make it all the way to her parents' cabin on Deck 9.

CHAPTER 24

Savannah taps quietly on the door. "Mom, it's me."

The door flies open. Savannah's mom hugs her and pulls her inside. Savannah grabs my arm as she goes, so I'm pulled in, too. I stand awkwardly to the side as both parents embrace her.

"Where have you been? We were worried sick. Are you okay?" her mom says with a break in her voice. She holds Savannah's face and examines her.

"Where'd this little boy come from?" says her dad, giving us both a stern look.

"I found him on the beach. Dad, he was all alone." Savannah hugs the boy tighter to her chest. "I think his parents are dead. Can he stay here with us?"

With all of us looking at him, the kid starts bawling.

"What are we going to do with a little brat?" her dad says, but he doesn't sound that upset.

Savannah's mom pushes him away. "Shame on you, Ryan. Let's get this little guy some cereal and milk."

"Why were you on the beach? Is Nolan with you? His parents are worried sick. He didn't come home last night either," her dad says, looking at me again with a frown.

"He should be back in his cabin by now," she replies and glances at me.

"We just talked to Nolan's parents. They haven't seen him since yesterday," says Savannah's mom.

"We were coming back from Kiribati, where we found the boy," I tell him. "By the time we got him up the ladder, Nolan and my brother were already up and gone. They're armed and know how to use the shotguns."

"Shotguns!" exclaims her mom.

"Maybe you'd both better start from the beginning," says Mr. Smith. Relief and anger mingle in his expression.

"Okay, but we don't have much time," I say.

Savannah does most of the talking, telling them the incredible tale as fast as she can. Before she finishes, Nolan and Jack show up. They're breathless with excitement.

"Look, Charlie, look what we've got," Jack says. They hold up walkie-talkies.

"Here's one for you, too, Charlie," says Nolan.

"They're Nolan's. We got them from their room. Guess what these can do, Charlie?" says Jack.

I'm relieved to see them. On the other hand, I'm also ticked off because they worried me. "Gee, I don't know, maybe communicate with someone?"

"Sheesh, Charlie, you don't have to be that way," says Jack.

"We got back to the ship, and you were gone," adds Savannah.

"Oh, we heard something and freaked. We started running down the halls and couldn't stop ourselves."

"Probably thumping along like rhinoceroses," I say.

"No, we were completely silent. Just like ninjas going down the hall," says Nolan.

"Yeah, we were ninja assassins going after our prey," adds Jack.

"And?" I ask.

"And what?" Jack says.

"And where did you noisy ninjas go?" I ask again.

"To Nolan's cabin to get these," Jack says, holding up the walkie-talkies, "but don't you want to know what they can do?"

"Yes, of course, Mr. Ninja Assassin. What can they do?"

"They call the zombies," says Jack.

"Yes," adds Nolan excitedly, "They lure the zombies from wherever they are."

"How did you find that out?" I ask.

"Well, we were going down the hall to our room when Nolan accidently hit the alarm on one. We panicked and dropped it. *Listen!* The zombies went for the walkie-talkie! We hid in a bathroom for a long time, until the alarm cut off, and then we went back for it," says Jack.

"That could be very useful," I say, then add, "Nolan, do you mind if I borrow them?

"No. I'll keep one. You can have the other three. But where are you going?"

"Jack and I need to go and get our parents out of their room." I grab my pack and put my hand on the doorknob.

"Where do you think you're going, Savannah?" says her dad as she moves to follow me.

"We've got to save the ship," she replies.

"You're not going anywhere, young lady," says her dad severely.

"But, Dad . . ."

"No. Absolutely not. You're grounded. You will stay here with us until I tell you differently. Is that understood?"

"We're not losing you again," adds her mom nervously. She pulls Savannah close.

"Nolan, I'd better take you to your room," says Mrs. Smith.

"We'd better go. My parents will be very worried, sir," I tell Savannah's dad.

"I'll come with you, Charlie," says Mr. Smith. "Savannah, hand me those guns." He takes the shotguns one at a time and checks that they're loaded. Savannah hands over the rest of the ammunition.

"Better take a crowbar, too," says Jack to Mr. Smith.

Savannah's disappointment at being left out shows on her face, but she doesn't protest.

Together, the three of us leave the cabin and take the stairs up one level to Deck 10. The body that was here yesterday morning when we left for Kiribati is gone. Uh-oh, it's not even twenty-four hours later. They're reanimating even faster than I'd thought. We quietly make our way to my parents' room, and I pry the remaining two nails from the doorframe while Mr. Smith and Jack keep watch. My parents pull us into the room and into a big family bear hug.

"Charlie, we were so worried. What happened?" says Mom.

"I want to hear it all, son," says Dad. "I'm sorry I didn't believe you."

"No, I'm sorry I locked you in here," I say and look away. It seems such a nasty thing now. I can hardly believe I would have done that.

"Come here, kid," Dad says as he wraps his arms around me again. "It's okay, you're back safe. We'll sort this out together."

Once again we tell the story of the last few days. I start from the very beginning this time, from when I saw Harry on stage. When I finish, ending with the rescue of Savannah and the little boy from the beach, I'm yawning. Must be late by now. At some point Mom tucked Jack into bed, and he's sound asleep. I scratch my head and yawn again. Dad and Mr. Smith exchange glances.

"Charlie, why don't you grab a shower and climb into bed. It sounds as if you've been up for nearly three days straight," says Dad.

"You smell like a wild animal," says Mom.

"Let us hash this out for a while," adds Mr. Smith.

"Okay," I reply. I start stripping my clothes off on my way to the bathroom. I turn the water to its hottest setting and climb in. Once in clean clothes, I feel like I'm wading through syrup on my way to bed. I find I can't keep my eyes fully open. The adults are gathered around the table. They're still talking when I lie down.

"What now, Ryan?" Dad asks Savannah's dad.

"I don't have the slightest idea, Dave," he replies.

"How can we fight hundreds of zombies with three shotguns?" says Dad.

"Can't be done," I say, but I realize my mouth never moved. And then I'm asleep.

CHAPTER 25

DAY SEVEN

I wake up to the sound of Jack's chatter. He's explaining how he got coconuts down from a tree.

"Uh, yeah, well, I knocked down some coconuts, and they were like uh, wow, we got some coconuts 'cause I was like, awesome. They were like, you're awesome Jack and I was like, I already knew that."

Of course, since it's Jack, the explanation is accompanied by a physical recreation of the perfect pitch he threw to knock the first one down, complete with a balled-up sock in place of the rock he had thrown.

Mom sits at the table listening. Dad and Mr. Smith are gone. I close my eyes again and fall back asleep, only to be hit by a sock ball. I groan and roll over.

A flurry of socks hits me in the back—*thwack, thwack, thwack*. "Jack, knock it off," I mumble.

He collects the socks and changes his angle of attack, standing over me on the foot of the bed. The socks fly at me again, this time hitting me in the face, one after another. They stink.

"That's strike three. Yoooou're *out!*" he calls.

"No, *you're out,*" I say.

Mom snickers.

I plant my feet on either side of his and reach up and grab his shirt. I roll over, knocking him off his feet, and then pull him down onto the bed. I roll all the way over and try to put him in an arm lock. He squirms and fights. We roll onto the floor. He drives his fingers into my ribs, and I bring my arms down to block him and wriggle away from his tickling hand. After grabbing both his arms, I'm just forcing him flat on the carpet when Mom's fingers dig into the backs of my legs.

"Not my hammies!" I cry and twist away from her tickling.

She attacks my rib cage, and I curl into a ball as they both go at me. My feet, neck, ribs, and thighs all get it.

"Stop! Stop!" I cry. I'm breathless with laughter and defenseless at this point. They fall back and we all rest to catch our breath.

"Come get some breakfast," says Mom. "We have milk and juice, bananas, cereal and toast."

"Toast?" I ask.

"Yeah, my hairdryer is exceptionally hot. It works just fine as a toaster. Want some peanut butter on your toast?"

"I'll take it all. I'm starving."

I go to the bathroom and come back to the sound of the hair dryer and a table full of food.

Mom smiles happily at me as I eat. "I'm so glad you're safe," she says. I smile back. "Where's Dad?"

Worry creases her face. "He and Mr. Smith went to fight the zombies," she says.

"What? Not just the two of them?"

I look around. Our packs are still here, but the shotguns are missing.

"They were going to find some other guys to help first."

"There's not enough ammunition to kill all the zombies on board. There must be hundreds of them now."

"What's their plan, Mom?" asks Jack.

"They'll start at the top and work their way down," she says.

Once they start shooting, all the zombies on board will be attracted to the noise. They won't be able to fire fast enough to keep up. They'll be overrun. "It's a suicide plan," I say.

Mom's face scrunches up in distress. "I told him not to go, but they said it's been too long since you all were on the sat phone. They don't think anyone is coming. They felt like they had to do something!" She's near tears.

"Mom, it's okay," says Jack.

"We'll make it okay," I add. Ever since Jack and Nolan came back with the walkie-talkies, a plan had been forming in my mind. With my thoughts elsewhere, I stare blankly at the wall. All at once, I can see how it might be done. We'll need the walkie-talkies, and some luck, to make this work.

"I think I can get them," I say.

They both look at me. "What are you talking about? The men took the shotguns," says Jack.

I look in my pack. "I've still got this M9 I got off of the dying officer. Besides, there's more guns on board."

Ships like this one always have a supply of guns because of the threat of pirates. Also, you never know when there may be a criminal on board.

"Where?" Jack asks.

"They will be close to the bridge. Maybe in the captain's cabin or close to it."

"Charlie, you're not getting into a shootout with the zombies," Mom says. "They'll be drawn by the sound just like you're worried about for your dad."

"Okay. We don't need the extra guns anyway for my plan. They're just so that we can move around on the ship. I had an idea about the walkie-talkies. It'll be totally safe, Mom," I add, looking through my pack. In my mind, I'm already planning how we can get the rest of what we'll need.

"Let's hear it," she says, leaning back and folding her arms across her chest. I drag my mind back to the present and describe the plan.

When I finish, there's silence in the cabin. "Hmmm, I wonder if that would work," Mom says. "It's a rather elegant plan, Charlie."

"Sounds cool, can I help?" says Jack.

"It would take both of us," I say.

"Wouldn't the ship burn up?" Mom asks.

"The sprinklers took care of it down in communications," I say.

"Okay, let's give it a try," she says.

"We'd better hurry if we're going to be any help to Dad," I tell her.

"Okay, then get a move on," says Mom.

"Jack, check your pack. Empty out the food. Keep your weapons and any matches if you have them. We also need some rope," I say.

"Okay," he says.

I reorganize my pack, too. I slide my sledge hammer through a belt loop. I stuff the walkie-talkies and a couple T-shirts into my pack. There's a box of matches and some electrical tape on the floor. I get these as well.

"Let's go, Jack."

"Charlie, I can't let you go out there alone," says Mom.

"It's okay, Mom, we know how to handle them. We made it back okay the last time, right?"

I block her from the door as Jack grabs his walkie-talkie and pack and eases out. "We'll be back safe. I promise"

"No!"

"Stay here, we'll be back soon."

"Give me that walkie talkie, Jack," says Mom.

"Aw, Mom," he says as she takes it from him.

"Let's go," she says.

"What?"

"You don't think I'm letting my whole family walk out and leave me alone in here, do you? I'm going with you."

"If you're sure, Mom," I say.

"I'm sure."

"Here, Mom, better take a crowbar," says Jack as he hands it to her.

CHAPTER 26

We creep down our hall, alert for any sounds. We hear some zombies and make a dash for the stairs to avoid them.

A distant shot sounds. "They're starting already," I say. We need to get moving!" The three of us tiptoe up the stairs to Deck 12 and walk back to the stern.

"I'll go down the ladder and haul the gas cans back up. You brought some rope, didn't you, Jack?"

He holds up a length of cord. Good.

"You guys keep a lookout while I'm down there. Mom, do you know how to use that gun?"

"Yes."

"Try not to use it unless you have to. The noise will attract them."

"I know, Charlie," she says, "I'm not stupid."

"Well, keep your crowbar ready then, just in case. Make sure you crush the skull."

She just rolls her eyes.

"I've got my bat, too," says Jack.

I start down the ladder to the launch. I count the steps as I go until I'm all the way down. I climb quietly into the launch and pick up the gas cans and the emergency kit. I tie the rope to the handle of the cans and loop it through my belt in the back. I return to the ladder. It's much slower going back up. The cans are awkward and heavy and keep banging into my legs.

I find Mom at the top of the ladder, a zombie at her feet. Jack stands nearby. She's leaning over to grab it by the feet when she sees me.

"Charlie, can you grab the arms? I want to get it over the side."

"Wow, you got one!" Together we shove the thing over the railing.

"Yes, we heard it coming up the stairs," Mom says. "When it got close, I walloped it."

"Good job, Mom," I tell her.

"There was only one can of gas that was full, and the other one's only half full," I tell them. "That's not going to be enough. "We need more flammable liquid, and a lot of it."

"Charlie, this is a cruise ship. It's fully stocked with flammable liquids," says Mom.

I look at her and say, "I know the fuel tanks are huge, but I don't know how we can get the gas out of them."

"You're forgetting another explosive liquid that's a lot easier to find."

"Huh?"

"How about vodka?" says Mom.

"Vodka?" repeats Jack.

"Yes, vodka, rum, whiskey, take your pick. This deck is full of booze."

I look at the poolside bar. I can't help but smile.

"There are three different bars on this level alone," she says.

"Are we gonna make Molotov cocktails?" asks Jack.

"Yeah, I was thinking one giant Molotov cocktail," I reply. "We're gonna take out all the zombies in one big boom."

"How do we move all this?" asks Jack.

"Let's get a lounge chair and load it up," I pull a chair over and lock it fully open. We wrap dozens of liquor bottles in towels and stack them on the chair.

Now for the fireworks. There are three big crates on the upper deck near the running track that are ready for the New Year's Eve celebration. We climb the stairs to the crates. I crack open a crate with Mom's crowbar. Wow.

"This ought to be enough gunpowder to light this place up," I say.

We pull out the biggest of the explosives and fill our packs, then stuff firecrackers down behind them. We go back down to the lounge chair.

It's heavy, but Mom and I each take an end and lift.

"Can I take point?" says Jack.

"No," I say.

"Come on, please?"

"No!"

"He'll have to," says Mom. "We've got our hands full here, Charlie."

"Woo-hoo!" says Jack.

We carry all the booze and then the gas cans to the elevator. Jack says, "If we go down to the theater from here, we'll be attacked as soon as we get off the elevator."

"I've got a diversion planned. Wait here. I'll be back in a minute."

I jog quietly past the wave pool to the forward elevators. I drag a lounge chair over to the elevator. I set a walkie-talkie to receive and tape it to the back wall of the elevator. I press the button for the theater level, prop the chair in the elevator so it leans against the door as it closes, and step away. The door slides shut. When the elevator gets down to the theater deck, the lounge chair will fall through the opening and hold the door open.

I hurry back to Mom and Jack and pull out my walkie-talkie. "Here, Jack," I say, "Call the zombies."

"Cool," he says.

He thumbs the talk button and says, "He-e-e-re, zombies, zombies, zombies," in a singsong voice.

We load the chair and packs onto the elevator while Jack announces in his best game show host voice, "Will all zombies please proceed to the elevator bay in the forward section. Calling all zombies to the forward deck."

As we urge Jack onto the elevator, he continues in his announcer's voice, "There will be zombie bowling and other activities starting in just a few minutes. Please move to the forward area." We close the doors and press the Stop button.

Mom checks her watch. "That should be long enough," she says.

"Okay, zombies, that's all I've got," Jack says. He turns off the walkie-talkie and hands it back to me. We press the elevator button for the bottom deck and start down.

If this works, the zombies will follow the sound of his voice to the forward lobby while we slip across the rear lobby and into the theater.

When the doors open, it looks as if the plan has worked. We step into an apparently empty lobby. The eerie sound of dozens of moaning monsters floats to us from down the hall.

"Let's hurry," Mom whispers.

Mom and I grab the chair and move to the double doors. The poster of Harry still hangs to the left of them.

"Look out!" cries Jack. I drop my end of the chair and duck. Jack swings his bat into the zombie. It drops in a heap, and we continue safely into the theater.

When we close the door behind us, the theater is black as night. Listening hard for shuffling footsteps, I grope for the light switch and turn on the chandelier overhead. A quick look confirms the theater is empty. No reason for them to come in here, I guess.

We lock the door, stand silently, and look around. The ceiling arches twenty feet above us. The crystal chandelier lights the space with a warm glow. The heavy carpet muffles our steps as we walk down the center aisle to the stage. On either side of the aisle are upholstered seats packed in tight rows. There's an orchestra pit in front of the stage, which is several feet below the level of the main floor. Cords pull the velvet drapes to each side at the front of the stage, and a system of guy wires with ropes and pulleys hang above.

"It might work," I say, looking around. "If we can lure the zombies in, they'll be funneled down this aisle to the stage. We'll suspend one bomb from the chandelier and the other over the stage."

"Look at this," calls Jack, who is nowhere to be seen. A square of the stage floor disappears, and Jack's head pops out.

"Cool," I say and climb down to him. He stands in a small room under the stage, barely inches taller than I am, which connects with the corridors outside the theater. A lever on the ceiling next to the trap door opens it. The door snaps closed quickly when the lever's released. "We can use this," I say.

"We need to get to work, boys, it's getting late," says Mom, looking at her watch.

I leave one gas can under the chandelier and put the other one on the stage. After unwrapping the liquor bottles, I top the gas cans off with alcohol. An alcohol and gas mixture will be just as explosive as the gas alone.

Jack pulls out a box of nails and empties them into the cans, then tosses in some firecrackers for good measure. He lays a box of matches and two full vodka bottles with T-shirt fuses on center stage. The rest of the fireworks he tosses around the room, concentrating on the aisle. Mom soaks two towels with alcohol and hands them to me, then pours the rest of the booze around the auditorium. I shove the wet towels half into the gas cans and throw a rope over the chandelier. I pull the first gas can about seven feet overhead, tie it off on one of the chairs, then go to the stage to raise the other can high above center stage. Mom sets up a microphone on a stand on-stage, plugs it in, and flips the switch. After tapping lightly to confirm it works, she flips it off and looks at me. Hands on hips, I turn slowly and survey what we've done. The room is ready.

We gather the rest of our supplies and carry them under the stage to the exits near the corridor. I pause in the relative safety of this space. I'm nervous about the next part. To Mom and Jack I say, "Let's go over this again and make sure we've thought of everything."

They nod, and we return to the stage. We talk through it slowly, trying not to miss any detail.

"Jack will have to be on-stage," Mom says. She adds, "You can be underneath to open the trap door, and I'll go to the stairs."

I look at Jack more closely, I think, than I have for a while. He only turned twelve last month, but he isn't such a little kid anymore. He stands nearly five feet five. His shoulders are broad and well developed from those endless hours playing baseball. He tosses an empty bottle easily from hand to hand, his weight balanced evenly on the balls of his feet.

"Okay, Mom," I say finally. "Here are the walkie-talkies." I hand one to each of them. "You don't have to do this, Jack."

"I'm good," he says and smiles. No stage fright for him.

"Take this, too, just in case," I say and hand him his bat.

Mom picks up a crowbar and heads up the center aisle to the lobby.

With my stomach churning, I leave Jack standing on the trap door and relock the doors behind Mom.

"Rock it, Jack," I say.

He flips the switch on the mike and lifts the walkie-talkie. He sings "Take me out to the ballgame" at the top of his lungs into them both. Through the doors of the theater, the sound echoes faintly.

If everything is going according to plan, then Mom has placed the other walkie-talkie in the stairwell. After she turns it on, she'll get out of the way. The sound of my brother's horrible singing should pull the zombies down the stairs towards the theater. The microphone blasting sound out of the theater should lead them right to us and pile them up outside the theater doors.

It's working. Already I can hear moaning from the lobby and the sound of dozens of shuffling feet. I give Jack a thumbs-up and hurry to my place below the stage.

Above me, Jack announces, "This next one goes out to all of you zombies out there. It's titled, 'Weasel-Stomping Day'." I grimace as his voice lifts into the opening bars. Surprising he doesn't shatter the chandelier by his singing alone. With my hand on the lever to the trap door, I can see through a window into the theater and to Jack onstage. After two choruses of the weasel song, Jack sings, "Chaar-lie, you look quite down with your big sad eyes and your big fat frown. The world doesn't have to be so gray. All you have to do is put a banana in your ear. A banana in your ear . . ."

The zombies battering the doors, seem to like the "Charlie the Unicorn" song. The doors bulge inward and finally give way, and with them comes a flood of zombies. They surge forward, with more piling in behind them. So far, the plan is working. I try to count them but quickly lose track. They're trampling each other in their need to get to Jack. The aisle fills halfway down to the stage. Some are forced into the rows of seats by the pressure of those surging behind them. They're a solid mass of bobbing heads. My hand tightens on the trap door lever.

"Now, Jack! Do it now!" I scream as they reach the orchestra pit and tumble in.

He drops the walkie-talkie and then dives for the matches and Molotov cocktail next to him. The zombies fill the pit. The first of them reaches the edge of the stage when Jack lights a match and touches it to the T-shirt wick. He cocks his arm, winds up, and lets fly at the gas can suspended from the chandelier. *Bam!* A direct hit. He scoops up the other liquor bottle, lights the T-shirt, takes aim at the other suspended can of gas, and let's fly. Another perfect pitch. Both gas cans flare.

I yank on the lever so fiercely it breaks off in my hand. I stare at it dumbly. I claw at the short piece that's left, but there's not enough to grip. The zombies close in on Jack. I dive under the trap door, grab the edge of the door, and struggle to pull it down, putting my weight into it. Jack's shouts rise above the chorus of moans. *Oh, no!* My shoulders ache with the strain. Finally the trap door begins to give. I brace my feet against the stage above me, hanging upside down, and pull even harder. My wrist joints pop, and the metal cuts into my fingers, but the door finally gives way.

The trap door flies inward. Jack and several zombies follow it. Jack swings his baseball bat even as he falls. When the door snaps back into place, it traps the arms of others of the undead. Jack takes out two of them before I'm back on my feet. I launch myself at the third one, clench its neck, and crack its skull on the hard wooden floor. I stand up, gasping for breath. A deafening blast rocks the auditorium—and then another one. *It worked!*

The tight space under the stage is becoming unbearably hot and starts to fill with smoke.

"Come on, Jack!" My arms searching blindly in front of me, I stumble through the smoke toward the exit. When I trip over something, Jack plows into me, and we nosedive into a tangle of rope. I get up and step blindly forward. The smoke is thick and getting blacker, making us cough and choke on it. Have we managed to burn down the whole ship? I pull the neck of my shirt over my nose and mouth and drop to hands and knees, pulling Jack down with me. I grope for the wall. The room has grown. We crawl endlessly without reaching its end. I'm

lightheaded, and my lungs burn. A faint glow of light pierces the murk. A silhouette appears in a doorway. We scramble toward it. Strong hands pull us out, and the door slams shut behind us.

"Mom!" I was never so glad to see anybody. "It worked, Mom!"

"Are you boys okay?"

All we can do is nod while we cough and rub our eyes.

"Zombies poured down the stairs and down the corridors. I hid in the ticket booth and watched. There were hundreds of them," she says with a shiver.

She hugs my little brother and says, "You did great, Jack."

"My first performance on stage, completely sold out."

I punch him in the shoulder.

"Ow!"

"Charlie, stop that!" Mom says.

I leave to check on the sprinklers.

It's still too hot to get near the theater, but even from the lobby the shushing sound of the sprinklers is obvious. The sprinklers are on in the lobby, too, and I'm drenched in no time. Flames cast a glow on the walls, and steam boils out the blackened doorway. Footsteps thump on the stairs. I don't have a weapon! I turn to run away.

"Charlie!" calls Dad, as he and a big man run down the steps. They stare into the burning theater. "What happened?" asks Dad.

"I laid a trap for the zombies. We lured them into the theater and then set off a couple bombs. It looks bad, but the sprinklers are putting out the fire."

"Whoa! Lucky you didn't burn up the ship," says the other man.

Dad pulls a fire extinguisher from the wall and sprays the flames. Now I can see piles of blackened bodies filling the theater but no sign of any movement.

"How many are in there?" Dad asks.

"Mom says she saw hundreds."

"Your mother?" asks Dad.

"Yeah, Mom brought the zombies down the stairs for us," I explain.

Mom and Jack come down the hall carrying the packs. "We did it!" Jack says when he sees us.

"So I hear," says Dad. "I'm glad you're all safe." He throws an arm around me and gives me a sideways hug.

Jack says, "I sang onstage until the theater was filled with zombies, and then I blew it up!"

"Wow! You did well, both of you," Dad says.

The other man says, "We were up on Deck 8, blasting away, but there were too many of them. We had to run and hide in a cabin. Then we heard the explosions, so we came towards the sound."

Mr. Smith comes down the hall, carrying a shotgun, with several others behind him.

They look into the steaming theater.

"What happened here?" says Mr. Smith.

With all of us standing there in the rain from the sprinklers, I tell them the whole story.

"Holy sh—!" one of the men says.

"Where's Savannah?" I ask her dad when I've finished.

"She's still locked in with her mom," he says. He looks more closely at us. "At least I hope she is."

One of the guys turns to Dad. "We walked through Deck 5 coming down here. No zombies anywhere. I think your boys got most of them."

All the men just stare at Jack and me and shake their head.

CHAPTER 27

The sprinklers seem to have put out the fire. We didn't get all of the zombies, though. A few drag themselves into the lobby as we talk. The men have no trouble shooting each one as it comes.

"It's not safe yet," says Dad. "I'll take you up to our cabins, and we'll work on a way to get rid of the last of them."

"That sounds good. I'd like to get into some dry clothes," says Mom.

We walk up to our rooms. Jack and I take our cabin, and Mom goes back to her room across the hall. We relax and rehash the excitement until she calls us to dinner. Dinner is peanut butter sandwiches, fruit, and cookies.

"If I never eat another peanut butter sandwich, it'll be too soon," says Mom.

We talk until Dad comes back.

As he eats, he fills us in. "We've cleared all of the upper decks, and we'll keep moving lower. We hope to be finished tonight. I'll be out late, but don't worry. Looks like you guys incinerated most of them. We're only finding an occasional zombie, mostly trapped in cabins, and they're easily taken care of. We're going room by room to make sure they're all gone."

"It only takes one to start it all up again," I say.

"Yep," he replies. "Charlie, you saved the ship today. I didn't want to say it earlier, but we were about to be overrun. We had no choice but to take them on, but there were too many. The sound of the gunfire drew them like moths to a flame. We couldn't have held out much longer."

I smile and sit up taller.

"I'm so proud of you," says Mom.

After Dad leaves, Jack and I go back to our room and turn in. An occasional gunshot pierces the night, but they are infrequent. Before long we fall into an exhausted but satisfying sleep.

CHAPTER 28

DAY EIGHT

The ship is silent when I wake. For once I'm up before Jack. I cross the hall to Mom and Dad's room and knock quietly. Mom comes to the door and gestures toward the bed, then puts her finger to her lips and steps into the hall.

"He's back," I say.

"Yes, they cleared the ship, and he only got back a couple hours ago," she says.

"The zombies are really all gone?"

"Yes. He said you could go down to Savannah's room this morning and let her know. And he'd like you to tell the passengers hidden in their rooms that it's safe to come out."

"Are any of the crew left alive?"

"I don't know. We'll find out today." She offers me cereal and milk for breakfast, but I'm not hungry yet, and I'd just as soon wait for something hot. I'm anxious to get going. Today is going to be a good day.

Back in my room, I shower and dress. I open the door and look down the hall, but hesitate in the doorway. The corridor is empty. I'm suddenly uneasy. In two strides I'm back in the room to grab my sledge hammer from the floor. I slide it under my belt and pull my shirt over it.

"See ya, Mom," I call as I leave. Whistling, I stroll down to Deck 9 and knock on Savannah's door.

The door flies open, and she throws her arms around me. "Charlie! You did it! Dad told me how you lured the zombies into the theater and then Jack blew them up."

"Yeah, well, he threw the Molotov cocktail, but it was all my idea," I mumble.

"It was brilliant! It was amazing!" She bounces, still hugging me. "I want to hear all about it." Her arms are tight around me.

I smile happily. I'm all fuzzy on the inside.

"I'm going to tell the passengers it's safe to leave their cabins. You want to come?"

"Sure, let me grab my shoes. Mom, I'm going around the ship with Charlie."

"Okay, but be careful."

As we walk side by side down the hall, I say, "So I'm not in the doghouse anymore?"

"Nope. They got over that real quick after you saved all our lives." She smiles at me.

I feel like I'm ten feet tall. My head should be bumping the ceiling.

I'm looking forward to this. After days of sneaking around because no one believed me and fighting zombies on our own, today I tell everyone how I saved the ship.

"Let's start on ten," I say, and Savannah agrees. We go to Lois's room first and knock on the door. "Lois," I call. "It's Charlie. It's safe to come out now."

"Charlie! Is it really? Oh, I'm so glad. I was worried sick. Hold on." The sound of nails being pried from the wood comes through the wall, and eventually the door opens. "Come on in and I'll make some coffee. You can tell me all about it."

"Uh, we can't," says Savannah. "We're telling all the passengers. We have a lot of rooms to cover."

"Oh, of course. So what happened?"

"Zombies took over the ship," I tell her.

"Zombies! I didn't think they were real. Are they all gone?" she says, looking both ways down the hall.

"Yes, almost all the crew was taken, but we lured them all into the theater yesterday, and I planted a bomb in there. You may have heard the explosion last night."

"How remarkable. I can't wait to hear all about it, but I won't keep you."

We say goodbye and move on. Mr. Schaefer in 1016 is still an old grump. He says he's going to call the captain and complain about kids running loose destroying things. Good luck with that.

The two old ladies next door to him don't seem to believe us, and neither do a lot of people. Finally, we give up explaining and simply tell them that it's safe to come out. Some of them are relieved that it's all over, but most of them are just mad. All of them say the same things. What's been going on? Why doesn't my phone work? Where is my steward? I haven't had a decent meal in two days. I want my money back.

"Savannah," I say, "These people are idiots. Everyone on board could have died and they're pissed off because they don't have room service."

"They're just scared and confused because life isn't what they thought it was. My mom's a nurse. She says when people get bad news, a lot of them act really angry instead of sad or scared like you'd think they would."

When we get to Deck 7, we see Jack, Nolan, and Truman way down the hall. They're going door to door as well. They seem to be enjoying themselves. Jack's doing a pantomime of lurching zombies. I take Savannah's hand. "Let's go get some food. They've got this."

We ride the elevators to Deck 12 and find the kitchen. "What are you in the mood for?" I ask as we explore.

"Whatever. A sandwich is fine," she says.

"Ugh, no more sandwiches for me." I pull out eggs, sausage, potatoes, cheese, milk, and juice.

"Tell me about home, Savannah," I say as I scramble the eggs.

She's sitting at a counter, watching me. "I live in Maryland, just outside of D.C."

"What's the best part about it?"

"There's great shopping in the suburbs and concerts in D.C. What do you miss most?"

I add some sliced potatoes to the skillet. I tell her about my home and friends. "Hey, tomorrow's New Year's Eve," I say. It dawns on me that we'll be going home soon.

"We should have a party," she says.

I scoop the food onto two plates. Savannah pours us some juice, and we dig in.

When we're both full, I say, "I think there's some fireworks left upstairs. Want to go look?" She says sure, and we head toward the elevators.

"There's still enough to make a good show," I say, looking through the crates.

"Isn't that the crew's job?" she asks.

"What crew?" I reply.

"How are we going to get home without them?" she asks.

"You're right, it's been too long since we called for help on the sat phone."

I look across the water at Kiribati. The island is full of movement, with the undead walking ceaselessly. Birds alight on them to feed and then soar to the sky again. There can't have been that many infected people on those launches. There must have been a lot of zombies thrown, or that jumped, overboard without being destroyed. They all seem to have ended up there.

"We don't have enough ammo to take them all out," I say.

"They sure spoil the view," she says.

"Let's go around to the bow where we'll see only the open ocean." We walk up to the bow and take the few steps to the bridge.

CHAPTER 29

The door to the bridge is unlocked. I open the door and speak over my shoulder to Savannah, "It'll be fun to have it to ourselves. Like we're in charge of the place."

"No, Charlie, look out! The captain and his crew are still here—"

Zombies crowd the room. I jump back through the door. One of the undead reaches for me. I pull on the door, but it's wedged open by a slimy arm. Other hands slip through the gap. I lean back hard on the door handle, struggling to close it. The door edges open. I've got my full weight straining on the door. A full chorus of hungry cries sends chills down my spine.

The gap widens. They're too much for me!

"Go for help, Savannah!"

"No way. I'm not leaving you."

"Okay, ready then?"

She nods.

I throw my weight into the door. It flies open, knocking them off balance.

I charge into the room, Savannah close behind. As I'd hoped, the zombies closest to the door have tumbled to the ground. They blunder to their feet. They close on me—all crew members. Their white uniforms are filthy with gore. I grab the sledge hammer from my belt and swing it axe-style into the nearest one's head. The head explodes with a wet sound.

Savannah lunges at what's left of the captain and rams her knife through his eye. He falls forward onto her, knocking her down. On her hands and knees now, she scrabbles for her knife. I edge around to stay between her and the others. I swing the hammer left and then right in a figure eight. Both blows connect with the skull of the next zombie. It falls hard. The last two are on me now, too close for the hammer. I raise my left arm and twist hard from the hips. I crash my elbow into the head of one. The impact shivers all the way down my spine, and I feel his skull give way. He falls forward onto me. His sudden weight takes me down. His body pins my legs to the floor.

Savannah screams.

He was a heavy guy, and I struggle to squirm out from under him.

It's too late. I've come up short. There's one left. It reaches for me. I can't find the sledge hammer.

I'm lost.

Suddenly I realize the body laying on me wears a security guard's uniform. My hands find his belt and the pistol holstered there. I rip the gun from the holster and thumb the safety lever off. I wonder if it's loaded. As the zombie leans down to maul me, I jam the muzzle against its rotting temple and squeeze the trigger.

Bam!

The last zombie drops on top of the first one.

The room is still. I take a deep breath and then wriggle my way free. I get to my feet. Savannah stands beside me.

I look around at the gory room. Blood and stuff I don't want to think about is splattered everywhere. But we're alive, and the bridge is ours. Through the bloody mess on the windows, the view is grand. I turn to smile at Savannah, but she looks back with horror in her eyes.

"Charlie, your shoulder," she says.

"What?"

"Your shirt is torn. Let me see."

I pull my sleeve up. There's a narrow scratch across my bicep. *Oh no!* I think, but say out loud, "It's not much."

"It's more than enough. Take your shirt off." She pulls out a pocket knife and selects a wicked-looking blade with a sharply pointed end. She pushes me down to the floor. "Charlie, try to hold still," she says as she brings the knife close.

"Savannah, what on earth are you doing?"

"I'm going to clean the wound and then suck out the poison."

I have a horrible vision of a chunk of meat missing from my arm and Savannah putting her mouth to the wound, sucking and spitting. I stare openmouthed at her.

"I saw that in a movie once for snakebite," she says.

"Ah, that's just a myth," I say. "It doesn't even work for snakes, let alone zombies." I push her hand away and get up. When I look at my arm again, my stomach sinks. I've been wounded by a zombie. I've got only hours left to live. My insides shrink, and I feel like I might throw up. I look at Savannah.

"Charlie, you're going to be okay," she says fiercely.

I try to smile, but it doesn't feel very natural. "Maybe. It looks like just a scratch. If no zombie blood touched me, I'll be fine."

"Let's at least get it cleaned up," she says and rips off the bottom of her shirt.

"Okay." But I know that if I'm infected, no first aid kit will ever do anything for me again.

Savannah gets some soapy paper towels from the bathroom outside the bridge. She scrubs the cut, then covers the wound by wrapping a strip of her shirt around my arm and tying a knot in it.

As she fusses with my arm, I examine the bridge around me. It's a long and narrow room, with wraparound windows overlooking the sea. Even through the gore, the view is grand. Banks of control panels are clustered in the center and at the far edges where the room stretches out to the sides of the ship. Most of the ship's controls form a large semicircle of workstations around the helm in the center. I'm surprised to see all the panels are lit up.

The bridge stretches out emptily to both sides of the ship, with lonely sitting areas complete with sofas and tables halfway along. At the far ends that stick out over the sea are smaller workstations.

We've done it. We've taken back the ship, against all odds.

I look at the bodies lying around. "Savannah, let's get these guys out of here."

We grab them by ankles and wrists and pull them out of the bridge and over to the rail and dump them overboard. It's an unpleasant task as they've been dead for days. When we dump the last one over the side, Savannah looks down at the bloody grime on her shirt and shivers.

"I'm going to get cleaned up," she says.

While she goes to her room to shower, I find bleach, rubber gloves, and a towel in the nearest kitchen. After washing up in the sink, I set to work cleaning up the bridge, starting with the workstations and finishing with the splashes of blood on the windows. Once it's done, I relax into the elevated captain's chair. To my left is a monitor showing a map, with our position marked. The chart table that stands behind the workstations has the same position marked. Looks like we're in the middle of nowhere. I trace the yellow line that lights up the monitor with my finger. It leads directly from our position across open ocean to Hawaii. The line ends in Honolulu, directly north of our current position. That was supposed to be our next destination before the cruise ended in L.A.

I spend the rest of the afternoon on the bridge. A trickle of people come and go, including Mom and Dad, who stay to talk for a while. Mostly I have the place to myself. Savannah brings a book up and settles on one of the sofas to read while I explore.

There's a cabinet full of manuals that describe each of the control panels around me. I pull out the first one and start reading. I find out that the central panels house the voyage management system, or VMS, which can be used to plot a course and keep track of the ship's position. Then there's the DPS, or Dynamic Positioning System. That's the ship's autopilot and navigation system. It links the GPS to the ship's maneuvering controls. Between the captain's chair and the pilot's chair opposite it, stands the helm with the wheel. I'm surprised to learn that the ship can also be controlled with a joystick built into the arm of the pilot's chair. How cool is that? I think to myself, sinking into the chair and moving the stick. Whoa, did the ship just move? I take my hand off the stick and gingerly climb out of the chair.

CHAPTER 30

The sun has dropped lower in the sky when I reluctantly leave the bridge. My stomach growls, and I realize I haven't eaten for hours. Downstairs, I find the ship transformed. Compared to the silence of the halls before, now the ship is alive with voices, with passengers moving through the ship and chatting in the lounges. I follow my nose to the dining room on Deck 8 and pass through it to the kitchen. My mom and Lois are there with some of the other women and even some uniformed crew I'm surprised to see.

"Hi, Mom. What's for dinner?" I say.

"Spaghetti and garlic bread," she says.

"Not quite what we're used to," I reply. I try to look into one of the steaming pots on the stove, but she bumps me out of the way.

"Not yet. Go out to the dining room and sit with your Dad. Unless you want me to put you to work."

"Nope."

Dad sits with Mr. Smith, together with some others I don't know. They've pushed two tables together to have enough room for all of them. I recognize the tall guy from down our hall as Ken Malone, who was there last night with Dad after the explosion. Mr. Malone leans to the side with one hand on his leg, with his elbow sticking out and knees spread as he talks, his voice as big as his personal space.

"You shudda seen 'em," he says. "We put one right into the brain, reloaded and blasted the next one behind him. Took both of us, taking turns, to keep up. We kept backing up until we had a whole pack of 'em laid out in front of us, like shooting ducks in a barrel." He barks a loud laugh.

"It's *fish* in a barrel, dude," says the heavyset guy next to him with a crooked smile.

"We need to find out how many zombies are left and how we get rid of them," says a broad-shouldered older guy in a clipped and nasal voice. I recognize Lars Thorwald, the jerk from our dinner with Nolan and Truman's family. He rubs his hand across his gray crew cut and then folds muscular forearms across his chest. He turns to the tall guy next to him and says, "How many did you see last night, Malone?"

"None. We got 'em all."

"Wonder how many passengers are left."

"I've got our passenger lists here, organized by deck," Dad says. "If I add the total for all decks, it looks like it comes to . . ." He looks at a clipboard, scribbles some numbers, and totals them up, but he's interrupted by a young guy with long hair.

"We've got to arm up and take the island," he says.

Ignoring him, Dad says, "We've got twelve hundred and fifty-eight passengers left on board, but there may be some we haven't recorded yet."

"Damn, that's a lot," says the fat guy. "How many were here to begin with?"

"No way to know, unless we find the ship's records somewhere," Dad replies.

"Sixteen hundred and seventy-two," I say.

"What?"

"There were sixteen hundred and seventy-two passengers aboard, according to the Ship's Guide," I say.

"It could've been a lot worse," says Smith.

"There were some kids that came by our cabin and warned us the night it all broke loose," says the heavy-set guy.

"Us, too," says Malone. "Spooked my wife so much we had room service and stayed in. We'd a been toast otherwise."

"That was me," I say.

They look at me in surprise. "Sure, I recognize you," the heavy guy says.

"Why don't you sit down, Charlie?" says Mr. Smith. He slides left so I can pull up a chair next to Dad.

"We need to stick to the subject here, gentlemen," says Thorwald. "We need to clear out the rest of the zombies on the island."

"So we can call for rescue," says the young guy.

"If we just sit tight, help will come," says Dad

"It's been two days since the kids used the sat phone," Mr. Smith says. "We can assume that help will not come."

"First off, we need to get to that phone," says the young guy. "My wife's pregnant and I'm gonna get her out of here."

"We gotta clear the zombies out," Malone says.

The heavy guy looks at him and says, "Okay, smart guy, how do we do that? I used my binoculars and counted the zombies over there. I gave up at fifty."

"We've only got a couple dozen rounds of ammunition for the shotguns," says Dad.

161

The young guy says, "We'll have to go in and fight hand-to-hand."

"But there's too many of them to fight hand-to-hand and anyway, the wiring to the satellite dish is toast," I tell them.

Malone says, "We could take a couple of the launches to different sides of the island. Split 'em up first, you know. Then go in with guns and clubs. I can fix the wiring."

"Several men in each launch would have to take out ten times their number," says the fat guy.

"Doesn't sound like good odds to me," says Smith.

"We've got no choice," says the young guy.

I'm tired of hand-to-hand combat with zombies. I'd rather find another way to get out of this. I get up and look out the window at the sunset, as they continue to circle around the same idea. How to get out of here? I ask myself. An idea nags at me, but I can't quite put my finger on it.

I walk back to the table and say, "Did anybody try working on the communication's system on board?"

"Oh, it's a mess down there," says Dad.

"I'm going down for a look," I say and start out of the dining room.

I can't help but be nervous as I walk through the ship. These halls were so recently echoing with moans and the sound of shuffling footsteps. I feel silly doing it, but I pull the sledge hammer from my belt and keep it at the ready as I go. The crew levels are a ghost town, however, and there are no undead left to lurch around the corners anymore.

I reach the communications room unmolested. Before even entering it, I see that it's hopeless. The whole place is a soggy, blackened wreck. I grab a handful of wires from a panel near the door. They're fused and break off in my hand. This won't work, I think. I'll have to find another way. I mull over the possibilities as the elevator takes me back to the dining room.

CHAPTER 31

I sit down to eat with my family, but my heart's not in it. There's a lump of dread in my stomach that won't go away. Kiribati's a death trap now. We're much better off working on the ship. No matter how much I tell myself that no zombie blood ever touched me, the worry of it also pulls at me.

After dinner, I feel sick to my stomach. I'm weak and woozy. Fear shoots through me. It's been hours since my fight on the bridge. I'm infected—I know it.

I leave the group and go out on deck. Gazing at the starlight reflected off the sea, I realize what I need to do. Savannah finds me there.

"What's the matter, Charlie?" she asks.

"Savannah, I need you to do something for me."

"Yes?"

"I want you to lock me in one of the cabins."

"Why? You're not thinking . . . just because of that scratch?"

"Yes."

"Oh, Charlie, no!" She throws herself into my arms and sobs against my chest. Jeez, she smells good. "Charlie, I can't let you go, not when we've come so far."

"Savannah, I'm sorry. Let's not make this any harder than it has to be."

"But, Charlie—"

My throat closes up and I struggle to speak. "Please," I say, and can't get anything else out.

"I won't," she says, her voice rough. She stares fiercely up at me.

Still hugging her tightly, I pause a long while to gather myself. "This is what I need you to do. I'm going down to my cabin. I want you to get a hammer and nails and lock me in there, just like we did to my parents, remember?"

"I don't want to," she protests. "I want to go with you."

"Savannah, if this is happening to me, I don't want to hurt anyone."

"How long do you have to be in there?"

"We should know by tomorrow morning. Send one of the men with a shotgun down tomorrow morning."

"Charlie, no, I can't," she says with fresh tears in her voice.

"Someone has to do it."

"Oh, Charlie."

"Let's go do this thing. No more talk," I say, my voice rough.

Eventually she nods against my chest.

I take a deep breath and hold it, then exhale slowly. I'll be okay now.

We pass through the main lounge. I find my mom and give her a kiss. "'Night mom, I love you."

She raises her eyebrows and gives me a quizzical look. "'Night, Charlie."

"G'night, Dad," I say.

"Goodnight, Charlie. I'm proud of you, son," he says.

I hurry downstairs to my room. Savannah comes with the tools and sits on the bed with me.

"You don't know there's anything wrong," she says.

"No."

"Probably you'll be just fine."

"Hope so."

"You saved the ship, you know. There's hundreds of passengers up there who wouldn't be alive except for you."

"Maybe so."

"You're a hero," she says.

I smile at her. "I'm glad I met you. Tomorrow, if I'm still here, would you like to go on a date with me?"

She smiles back through her tears. "I'd love to. I have a killer dress I haven't worn yet. Tomorrow is New Year's Eve, you know."

"Well, that's something to look forward to. We'll do it up right."

Her smile slips away and she kisses me, her lips soft on mine. An electrical charge shoots through me.

"Charlie, I—," she says, her cheeks glistening with fresh tears.

"Do it now," I say.

She runs from the room. The sounds of a hammer pounding and sobs come through the door.

I look around my prison. This really sucks. It's a stupid way to die. Suddenly I feel weak, and my stomach lurches. I lay my sledge hammer next to the bunk. I lie down and stare at the ceiling for a long time.

Eventually I say a silent prayer, and then I close my eyes and drift off.

Savannah lies in bed unable to sleep, then rises and carries a blanket and pillow up one deck and sits down outside Charlie's room. She puts an ear against the door, hugging her pillow, and listens, but hears nothing. After a while, she lies down across the doorway and stares into the darkness.

When it's finally morning, she goes to find help. A crowd soon gathers in the hall outside the locked door.

CHAPTER 32

DAY NINE

The sound of banging on the door rouses me.

"Charlie, Charlie!" my mother calls.

My head aches, and I put my hands over my ears. There's a sound of scraping, and the door creaks. Suddenly I remember and look at my watch. After six in the morning. I mentally check myself over: head, stomach, limbs. Everything feels normal. I don't feel any urge to rip into human flesh.

I stand and stare into the mirror over the desk. Eyes are bloodshot, but I don't *look* dead. I raise my arms awkwardly in front of me and try out a long moan. Halfway through I sneeze.

A pulse beats in my neck, and my cheeks are flushed. Nope. Not a zombie. All the tension goes out of my muscles. I'm okay! I rise and stretch and yawn, then open the door.

There's a whole crowd out there. Not just one of the men with a gun, but also my whole family and Savannah's.

I let the sigh linger in my throat. I feel a little playful. Keeping my face blank, I stare at the tense faces, enjoying their shock. My mom's face crumples, which makes me feel bad. When the barrel of the shotgun starts to rise toward me, I finally throw my arms wide and smile. "Good morning!"

Mom gathers me in a big hug. "My Charlie! How could you?" Dad embraces me, too, and Jack comes running and almost knocks us all over.

Savannah grabs me and kisses me on the mouth right there in front of everybody. It feels good. Jack makes loud smooching sounds. Laughter fills the hall.

It's all over, I think, until I remember we're still stranded in the middle of the Pacific Ocean, three thousand miles from the continental U.S. and five thousand miles from home.

CHAPTER 33

The whole crowd climbs into the elevator and we make our way to the dining room. There's a much smaller selection of food on the buffet than usual, but there's plenty of it. I find a table that looks out on the ocean and sit down to eat, Savannah next to me.

"What should we do today?" Savannah asks me.

"You know, I'd like to kick back and relax. How about some shuffleboard?"

"That'll be quite a change from the last few days."

"Yeah, that's the point. Sunshine, fresh air, and <u>no zombies</u>."

"Feels good, huh?" says Savannah.

"Yep. I've also got some planning to do for tonight," I say.

"What's going on tonight?" Mom asks from across the table.

"It's New Year's Eve," says Savannah.

"You're right. I totally forgot," says Mom. "I wonder if it would be appropriate to have a New Year's Eve party."

"Yeah, let's do it," adds Jack. "Fireworks and loud music. I could play the drums."

Mom says, "A lot of the passengers have lost loved ones, but it seems right to celebrate that so many of us are still alive." She turns to my Dad. "What do you think, Dave?"

But he's frowning and looking in the other direction.

He's watching the table of men over by the window. It's most of the same guys from yesterday, and they're getting loud. Did they sleep in the dining room, or what?

Thorwald leans forward and jabs his finger at Mr. Smith, who raises his hands defensively as he shakes his head.

"I think you could go ahead with it. Just nothing too wild," Mom says.

What? Oh, yeah, the party.

"Savannah, you ready to go?" I ask. She nods. "Okay, see you, Mom."

"'Bye, honey, so glad you're okay," she calls.

"Does she have to shout out *honey* like that?" I mutter to Savannah.

"Chill out, Charlie. That's what moms do."

"Guess you're right."

"I'll go get Nolan," calls Jack as he runs for the stairs.

"Just what we need. A pair of twelve-year-olds tagging along," I say.

"You don't like your family much, do you?" Savannah asks, turning to look at me.

"I don't like to be smothered," I say, covering my smile with my hand.

Savannah catches me at it and stops me with a look. "What is it with you today?"

"I'm trying to be the surly teenager, but I'm just not feeling it anymore."

"So what, this is just an act?"

I shrug and keep my face glum, but actually I feel pretty cheery today. Some of it must leak out my face, 'cause she punches me in the shoulder. Ow!

At the shuffleboard courts, we grab the sticks and pucks and start a game. It's a total yawn, but I'm cool with that today.

Before long, Jack shows up with Nolan and Truman. Truman runs to me and hugs my legs, "Hey, Charlie!"

I grab him around the knees and flip him upside down over my shoulder. "Hey, little dude," I say. I look at him upside down. His arms dangle.

"Dad says you're a hero and saved the ship! Are all the zombies gone now?" he asks.

"Yep. We blew them all up."

"Cool," he says.

"Except for the ones on the island. Dad says they're gonna go after them," says Nolan.

I put Truman down, and we line the pucks up on the shuffleboard grid. The boys can't seem to move without talking at the same time.

"So, Charlie, how should they kill the zombies on Kiribati?" asks Truman.

"Can we take a break from the zombie talk?" I say.

"Hey, this would work. We could light Molotov cocktails and slide them towards the zombies," Jack says and demonstrates with the shuffleboard stick.

"Oh, yeah," agrees Nolan.

"No, they wouldn't explode," I say. "You have to break the bottle for it to work. And anyway, a Molotov cocktail by itself isn't enough to kill a zombie. You've got to have enough heat to melt its brain."

It's my turn, so I grab the long stick and slide the puck down the deck just as Jack says, "Hey, what about a chainsaw? I'd be like *brrrr* and *vroomvrrooooooom-vroom*, slash up, slash down, slash their heads off."

My shot goes wide. "No, that's a really stupid idea," I say. "The noise attracts them, and it would splatter blood everywhere." I scowl at him. "You messed up my shot, jerk."

"Yeah, and where are you gonna get a chainsaw on a cruise ship?" says Nolan.

"There's got to be one. How else do they carve the ice sculptures?" says Jack.

"Right," says Nolan sarcastically.

"Come on, it might happen," Jack says. "You might get attacked carving an ice sculpture and have to cut a zombie head off," says Jack.

I sigh. Here we go again.

"My dad says they're gonna go to Kiribati and call for help," says Nolan.

"You already called," I say.

"He says they must not have believed me, and if anyone was coming, they'd be here already." Nolan looks pensive.

"It *has* been a while," Savannah agrees.

It may take more time before help arrives. We're late for our stop in Hawaii, but we're not expected in L.A. until tomorrow. They may need another day to find us.

Wonder how long the food will last? Ships like these usually restock food and water at each port. Could be a diet cruise before we get off. I smile. That would be a good change. Get the oldies to slim down some.

We'll run out of water before that, though, and that's a bigger problem. There are fewer people on board now, so that will help.

"What do you think they're going to do?" Savannah says.

I set down my stick. "I'll ask my dad what's going on," I say with a sigh, and leave them there.

The dining room is filling up for lunch, but I find Dad still there, sitting with the group of men against the far windows. Nolan's and Savannah's dads are there, too, along with all the rest of them from before. Crumpled paper coffee cups and dirty plates litter the table.

Mr. Smith sees me as I walk toward them, and his expression lightens. "Charlie, come on over here. We're working out our strategy."

I take an empty chair and look around the table. Thorwald and the young guy huddle at one end, talking in voices too low for me to hear. At my end the three dads sit, with Mr. Malone in the middle between the two groups.

"We just charge in and take 'em out," says the young guy.

"I fought terrorists in the desert. I can take out zombies on the beach," says Thorwald.

"Lars, you can't just take them out the same way you're used to," says my dad. "You have to get their brains. They'll just keep coming at you if you don't."

"Not man enough for it?" says Thorwald. "We can do this alone. You don't need to be a part of it." His chin sticks out, and his expression is mocking. The dude is like sixty. What is his deal? He have a testosterone sandwich for lunch every day?

"It only takes one bite and you're infected," my dad says. "You'd be back on the ship and reanimated a day later, and then this whole thing starts right up again."

"Listen, we've got some military experience around this table," says the young guy, gesturing around the table.

"Fine," says my dad and gets up to leave.

"Listen, I'm a veteran, too," Mr. Hoskinson says, "and this is not the right way to go about it." He gets up, too.

I follow them. "What are they planning?" I ask.

"They don't know yet. Everybody has a different idea. They just go around and around in circles. Some military experience," Dad says.

"What do you think we should do, Dave?" Mr. Hoskinson asks my dad.

"If we wait here long enough, either help will come because of Nolan's calls or because we haven't shown up when we were supposed to."

"So we just need to stall now?" I say.

"Yes. If only that bloody island weren't so close, there'd be no question about it."

I get a sandwich and drink from the buffet before I leave. I take my food back to the shuffle board court. Savannah and the boys are gone, though, so I wander back up to the bridge. Sitting on the wing of the bridge overlooking the island, I munch on my food and think about the zombies. How will those zombies be exterminated? Someday, someone can come back and kill them off, but how will they ever find the ones that wander into the ocean?

I'm sick of zombies, sick of fighting them and sick of thinking about them. I'd much rather learn more about the bridge. This is a once-in-a-lifetime opportunity, and I have it all to myself. I pick up the books and start reading.

"The Pacifica is a seventy thousand ton ship," I read. "Passenger capacity eighteen hundred. Staffed by six hundred crew members." Unbelievable. Out of them only sixteen survived. We're lucky most of the passengers made it. She can cruise at a speed of twenty-five knots. I search my memory. I'm not sure, but I think that's around thirty mph. Doesn't seem very fast.

At that speed how long would it take us to get to Honolulu? I ask myself.

I go to the chart table. It's a six-foot-long table with a giant map attached to its top. I find drawing tools in a drawer. I double-check our position on the VMS monitor, then mark our position with a red "X" on the map. I mark another "X" over Honolulu, Hawaii, then use the yardstick to measure the distance between them.

Using the key on the chart, I do the math. We're about nine hundred miles from Hawaii. At thirty mph, that means we're thirty hours away. That's just a day and a half. California is much farther, more than three thousand miles away.

Looking again at the DPS and all the other controls that are lit up, as if ready for the captain's orders, I wonder about the anchors.

I leave the bridge and walk the perimeter of the ship and look down the sides. Finally, I'm sure. All the anchors are snug to the ship. The ship is stationary without using them. Amazing. I go back to the bridge and look at the DPS manual again. Yes, just as I thought. The DPS, the autopilot, can be programmed to maintain the ship's position. No anchors needed. When I pay attention, I feel the vibrations of the engines firing up occasionally to keep us in place. Wicked.

But what if we run out of fuel? We could just drift forever. I consult the manuals and then look at the fuel gauge. Still more than half full, so no danger for now, but the DPS is only meant to be used for a few hours. It's been keeping us here for three days. I wonder how long the DPS can go. I spend a couple more hours studying the manuals before Jack shows up.

CHAPTER 34

"I thought I'd find you here," Jack says, stepping onto the bridge. "We need to get this party rolling."

"Okay," I reply. "Let's go get the fireworks."

The three crates we plundered earlier rest on the top deck overlooking the pools. Jack pulls out handfuls of roman candles and firecrackers and then increasingly larger packages.

"Wow, look at these!" he exclaims. "Vesuvius, Mountain Fountain, Mammoth Hot Java."

I look into the next crate and pull out the biggest so far, the Triple Nitro. There's a ridiculously large number of fireworks. We stack them on the deck and look at the darkening sky. Almost time. In the light from the setting sun, the undead cast long shadows on Kiribati. I shiver. I shake off the memory and go below with Jack to spread the word.

As a crowd gathers on the afterdeck, someone cranks up the stereo in the adjacent ballroom. Music floats out the open doors. Flashlight and matches in hand, Jack and I begin at one side of the deck by setting off tremendous strings of firecrackers.

Below us, people jump, and a few women scream. Laughter follows after the shock of it. We glide along the deck, matches lighting up roman candles, then ever larger rockets. The sky is alight with colors. Explosions fill the air. Triple Nitro explodes last—a soaring spray of twinkling gold and silver lights. Jack sets off one final string of fireworks to accompany it. The crowd exhales a last "Ah, ooh," and the fireworks echo into oblivion.

Downstairs, the music shifts into some old-style Motown, and the adults drift back indoors.

"Wicked show," says Jack.

"Yeah, pretty good," I reply.

We descend to the pool deck where the rest of the kids hang out.

"Let's go get something to drink," says Jack.

He strolls behind the poolside bar we broke into earlier and I follow. Was it only yesterday? All the alcohol got scavenged to burn the zombies, but the mixers remain.

Jack sets up two tall glasses and fills them with red juice, Seven Up, pineapple, and finally Pepsi, then tops it off with an umbrella.

"Here you go," he says.

I down the whole thing. It's fresh and sweet. I plunk my glass onto the bar. "Make me another, barkeep."

He does, and I drink again. A line of kids forms behind me.

"How about a kiddie cocktail?" Jack asks the boy behind me.

"Yeah," says the kid.

He sets him up with one, then eyes the girls next in line.

"Hiya, hot thangs," he says, and as they laugh he speeds into flashy high gear. His hands fly, and his head bops, and finally he places some ridiculous concoction in front of a girl.

"Sheesh, Jack, they're like eight," I tell him, but he's already on to the next girl.

I leave Jack to his bartending and find a lounge chair where I can watch the party. The smaller kids run screaming up and down the deck, and a bunch of tweener girls dance in one corner. The night has cooled off, and the moon is bright. It's good to be here. It's good to be *alive*.

A warm hand touches my arm. I look around to see Savannah. "Hey."

"I liked the fireworks," she says.

"You look great." And she does. Her eyes are dark and wide, and her blond hair falls in soft curls to her shoulders. The short red dress must be the one she mentioned. She twirls to show it off.

"Wanna dance?" she asks.

I don't dance. "Uh . . . ," I say.

She takes my hand and pulls me over to an empty corner of the deck. At least it's dark there, so no one will see me making an idiot of myself. Savannah puts my arms around her waist and drapes her arms around my neck. The music is slow, and I quickly catch on. All I have to do is shift my weight from one foot to the other. No problem. I rest my cheek on her head and pull her closer.

"Charlie, I'm afraid," she says.

"What's wrong?"

"I'm worried about my dad. Something's going on. He and my mom were whispering earlier. My mom's crying, and she won't tell me anything. I think he's going to do something stupid."

"Your dad's not a stupid guy."

"I know, but he feels like he has to help." I look down into her eyes. They're dark and shining in the dim light.

"He was in the Air Force for twenty years."

"Yeah?"

"He retired right before his unit went overseas for combat in Iraq. He feels guilty for getting out while a lot of his friends got injured or killed. I'm afraid he's going to get himself hurt."

"I'm sure you're wrong."

There's a long silence. Savannah's head droops, and her back feels tense under my hands. I squeeze her gently.

"I couldn't stand losing him," she says softly against my chest.

"Aw, you won't. We'll make sure of it."

"What are we going to do?"

"I'll go see what I can find out. You try one more time to talk some sense into your dad. I'll meet you on the bridge later." I lift her chin and say, "C'mon, don't worry. I'll take care of everything." She relaxes against me.

I leave her reluctantly when the song ends. I walk into the ballroom. The music hits me like a wall. The room is packed. Appears to be a successful old folks party. Oldies grooving to oldie music fill the floor. Everyone's got a drink in hand. As I wander through the crowd, my brother's voice rises above the noise. Is he everywhere?

"Call your peeps, 'cause DJ Jack is in the house," he yells over the sound system. "We'll kick it off with some funky music. Here's a remix of Sylvester with his tune 'Do Ya Wanna Funk?'—going out to all my peeps in the hood."

The song pounds the air. I catch sight of my brother dancing behind the stereo setup. He's wearing sunglasses and his baseball cap backwards, gangsta-style. I shake my head. All the oldies seem delighted to groove to Jack's goofy song.

Finally I see my parents in the corner. They're watching Jack and smiling. I cut through the dancers to them. "Dad," I shout, "What's going on? What did you all decide to do next?"

"I couldn't stop them," he shouts into my ear. "Two boatloads of those idiots take off for Kiribati tomorrow at dawn. They'll charge in with crowbars and Molotov cocktails and lock themselves in the building until help arrives."

"That's a suicide mission! The Molotov cocktails probably won't kill the zombies," I say. "Can't you stop them?"

"No, I'm on the outs. The young guy has convinced them they've got to get help. Lars and Malone are convinced they're the military experts and won't listen to anyone else."

"Are Nolan's and Savannah's dads going, too?"

"Probably."

"You won't go, will you?"

"No, I think it's a stupid plan."

"Good. It is."

"We just need more time."

"We've got to do something to stop them," I say.

"Why don't you work some of your magic, Charlie?"

"I'll see what I can come up with."

I work my way through the crowd and drag Jack away from the music, then find Nolan.

"What's up, Charlie?" Nolan says.

"Nolan, your dad is going to Kiribati tomorrow morning. We're going to stop him"

"What do you mean?" Nolan says. Some screaming little kids run between us.

This is too wild. "Follow me."

We walk to the forward stairs and climb up to the bridge, where it's quiet, cool, and dark.

CHAPTER 35

Jack, Nolan, and I settle on the sofas mid-bridge.

"Listen, we've got to do something to stop them from going," I say. "A full-out attack won't work. There's not enough ammo.

Savannah comes in and slumps into a chair.

"No luck, huh?" I say.

"No. My dad won't even talk to me about what's going on.

We sit in silence, slumped in our seats. I can only think of one way out of this. We have to get farther away from the island. Eventually, it's too much for Jack and Nolan. They start bumping each other. They're working themselves up to a wrestling match when I say, "Why don't you guys get us something to eat? I need to think about this some more."

"Okay, we'll be right back."

"Take your time."

Savannah stays slumped in the chair, staring blindly out at the night. Her eyes are red, and she looks exhausted. The noise of the party drifts up to us. She checks her watch and says,

"Midnight already. Happy New Year. We don't have much time to figure this out."

"Don't worry," I say. "I'll take care of it. I promise."

Savannah's mouth stretches into a big yawn.

"I'll stay up. I have some work to do. You sleep," I tell her.

She comes to me and puts her head on my shoulder. I stroke her hair gently as I stare into the dark. After she's asleep, I slip from her embrace, get up, and study the controls.

I check the fuel gauge, then our position on the DPS. I sit in the captain's chair and stare out at the empty ocean. If we were farther from Kiribati, there'd be no choice but to wait for help. I look at the map on the monitor and trace the yellow line that marks our route to Honolulu programmed into the VMS.

Finally, I'm ready.

CHAPTER 36

It's crazy, what I've decided to do.

I'll engage the DPS, and it will start the ship on the route to Hawaii. After we're out of sight of Kiribati, we'll shut it down and wait. By the time everyone wakes up, the island will be gone. Excitement stirs in me. I can barely resist the siren song of the ship's controls. I pace nervously until Jack and Nolan come back. I'm too worked-up to eat.

We wake Savannah, and I explain my plan. They're wide-eyed with surprise. My intensity surprises even me. Crazy as it seems, I think I can do this.

"If you've completely thought this through, then walk us through it step by step," says Savannah. "Don't leave any detail out."

I explain the DPS, how it's kept our position here for so long. Then I show them the course programmed into the VMS to take us back to Honolulu. I explain everything I know about all the systems on board. It must be pretty convincing, because at last they agree.

"We're going to need the walkie-talkies," I say. While the boys go get them, I pace in front of the controls. Finally, they're back.

"Nolan, take a walkie-talkie down to the engine room."

"Aye-aye, Captain," he says and runs out.

I grimace nervously at his back as he goes. I send Jack to the bridge wing to check the propellers. I look through the windows, then at the ship's clock. Two A.M.

Sitting in the pilot's chair, I look at Savannah. "What do you say?"

"Go," she says firmly.

I press the button to switch the DPS to the highlighted route. The button flashes red until I press it again. Just like the manual says, the light turns green. The DPS route should be activated now. Will it work? The vibration of the engines increases.

"Savannah, watch the warning lights," I say, pointing to the panel on my right.

"What could go wrong? How much fuel remains?"

"More than half a tank. Enough to make it back to Hawaii, I think."

"It'd be better if we were in more populated waters so rescue would be more likely if something happens," she says.

I nod.

"We'll cross a major shipping lane on the route that's plotted. See how it's marked on the chart table?" I say. "If we start on a VMS-plotted course and follow the yellow line, like the yellow brick road, then maybe we can signal another ship, find another place on the way to get help."

"That would be great."

"How's everything look?"

"No warning lights," she says.

Jack looks down at the water from the port wing. "Are the propellers moving?" I call to him.

"Uh, maybe," he says, then adds a moment later, "Yes! I can see the water churning."

"Go out on deck and see if you can tell if we're moving away from the island," I tell him.

I pick up a walkie-talkie and say, "Nolan, how's it look in the engine room?"

"It's really noisy, seems like it's the engines, but everything looks okay."

I perch in the pilot's chair with my hand near the joystick, but very carefully don't touch it. I get up and stand behind the helm, look out at the dark horizon, but don't touch anything there, either. The wheel turns on its own. I bounce on my toes. I pace. I stare intently at the controls. The manual says it takes six people to run this ship. Crap, what have I done? It can't be this easy.

"Charlie, a warning light came on," says Savannah.

"Uh-oh. What is it?" I ask, walking over to look.

"It's labeled 'ARPA.'"

I dig through the manuals searching for the right section. "ARPA, or Automatic Radar Plotting Aids," I read. "It provides information on positioning, distance, speed and other objects by connecting the ship's radar with the computer."

"Do you think that means we're off course?" She bites her lip.

"I don't know. The VMS still looks okay."

I run my finger along the yellow line on the VMS console. Are we moving? I check the map on the chart table. Our starting position is still marked. I'll wait an hour to mark a new position.

Jack runs back onto the bridge. "We're moving!" he shouts. "The island is getting farther away!"

Savannah rushes outside to look.

"Great. Keep an eye on it," I tell him.

An hour later I take a new reading from the VMS monitor and plot it on the chart table. I place my other finger on Honolulu and look at the distance between the two fingers. Savannah looks with me. "We're on the right course, but it's an incredibly long way to go," she says. "The ARPA warning light isn't on anymore."

I spend another hour nervously pacing around the bridge and looking at the controls. I page through all the manuals again to make sure I haven't missed something.

"Charlie, relax, everything seems to be going fine," says Savannah.

"This is nuts. What on earth am I doing?"

"You're just taking an eighteen hundred-passenger cruise ship on a nine hundred-mile journey across the Pacific. Piece of cake," she says.

"What are my parents going to say?"

"You'll be grounded for the rest of your life," says Jack. "Good thing I didn't have anything to do with this."

I smile at him, feeling giddy. "It's worth it. This is cool."

Another hour goes by. I look at the clock. Four A.M. Night surrounds us. Jack and Nolan sleep on the couches. Savannah yawns.

I look at the fifty or so miles we've covered on the VMS monitor. "We should be out of sight by now. I'm not sure I know how to reprogram a new stationary point, but the VMS is taking us to Honolulu."

She grins at me. "All right! That's going to be some surprise when everyone wakes up."

Another hour goes by. It's five A.M. and still dark outside. I plot our position, then draw a neat line between the points. We're sailing across the Pacific Ocean, directly to Hawaii.

I stand alone before the captain's chair. The sky lightens in the east, to my right. It's a beautiful dawn. The ocean is silvery, with small whitecaps. We watch a school of dolphins as the sun comes up.

"It's another beautiful day in paradise," I say. I pull a deep breath into my chest and exhale with a big sigh. It's good to be alive.

At six, I plot our position on the chart table. We've gone more than a hundred miles across the Pacific. Only eight hundred to go, I think, and stifle a hysterical laugh. At this pace, we'll be in Honolulu in twenty-six hours. Maybe we don't need to find help or civilization along the way.

"Could we just sail all the way into Honolulu?" I ask myself.

Savannah looks at me with surprise.

CHAPTER 37

DAY TEN

We're still feeling giddy when a half dozen men burst onto the bridge. It's the hotheaded group planning to fight it out on Kiribati.

Thorwald looms over me. "What in the hell is going on?" he shouts into my face. "Who do you think you are playing around up here?"

They all look angry and primed for violence. They must have been about to leave for Kiribati. They've got shotguns slung over their shoulders, and a couple of them carry heavy clubs, as well. There's so much shouting I have trouble understanding any of it. Thorwald grabs my arms from behind, wrenches them up painfully, and starts dragging me from the bridge.

"Lock him in his room and put a guard on him," he commands the others. Questions fly at me as we go out the door—"Where are we?" "How far are we from Kiribati?" "Are we drifting?"

My dad stands just outside the bridge. "Let go of my son!" Dad shouts. He grabs Thorwald's arm and tries to push him into the lobby. Thorwald shakes Dad off and glares at him. My dad is over six feet but is a toothpick compared to the old guy, who's got muscles bulging from his muscles.

Mr. Smith and Mr. Hoskinson come up behind Dad, blocking the way.

"Cool off, Lars. Let him explain," says Smith.

"Back off!" says Thorwald. The others gather behind him.

"Let's at least find out what's going on," says Nolan's dad.

"What's going on is the ship has drifted out to sea," Thorwald says. "This kid has been fooling around and gotten us lost in the middle of the Pacific! He ought to be strung up."

"Get your hands off my son!" shouts Dad and elbows his way between the two of us.

I stumble forward when Thorwald releases me. He shoves my dad in the chest. Dad staggers backward, but he stands his ground. Lars takes a boxer's stance and looks primed to throw a punch. Dad raises his fists. The men pull them apart.

Hoskinson steps between them. "Hold on, here. Before anybody does anything stupid, we need to understand what's going on," he says. "These kids saved us from the zombies. They deserve a chance to be heard."

"Charlie, explain why we've left Kiribati," Dad says.

"I was worried that Nolan's and Savannah's dads would be in trouble. You said it'd be so much better if we were out of sight of the island." They all stare incredulously at me.

"So you did *what*?" Dad asks.

Doubt floods through me. My excuse sounds so lame. What was I thinking?

Thorwald lunges for me. "I'll throttle him! He has no way of knowing where we're going. We could be heading straight west for all he knows."

I duck away from him and yell, "Look out there, you idiot." I point out the windows. "See the sun? What direction do you think we're going?"

"It's a big ocean," he says, blinking in the bright sunlight. "There's a lot of places we could end up that aren't Hawaii."

"Let me show you," I say and move toward the bridge, Savannah's dad clearing the way for me. "Here's our position. We're about one hundred and fifty miles north of Kiribati." I point to the chart table, where I've plotted our progress. A neat line connects my "X"s. Dad, Smith, and Hoskinson step forward and take a look. Tension fills the room.

"How do you know that's where we are?" says Dad.

"The VMS, over here." I point. "See, the course is plotted on this monitor."

All the men look at it.

"So the island's out of sight. Why not stop here?" Dad says.

"I'm not sure I can. I'd have to program in a new stationary site."

"You mean, there's no way to go back?" asks the young guy.

"Lock him in a room somewhere," Thorwald shouts. "This kid is out of control. He's a danger to the rest of us." He grabs me again and drags me toward the door.

"Who will pilot the ship then?" I shout back at the others.

"If you did it, so can I," says Thorwald.

"Oh yeah? Where's the fuel gauge? How much fuel is left? Where's the emergency stop? How will you navigate?" I struggle in his grip, but it's no use.

Savannah gestures at Thorwald. "Dad, make him stop. Let us explain."

"Hold on a minute, Lars. Let's think about this," her dad says.

"Let him go. What're we gonna do?" Malone says as he pries me from Thorwald's grip.

I straighten my shirt and stand by my dad. I turn to Thorwald, cross my arms, and say, "This is my bridge now, and I want you off of it." I wonder if I've pushed too far.

Luckily, Savannah's dad steps between us. "Come on, Lars. Let him be. Come outside and we'll talk."

"Back off, Smith. I want to hear this boy explain himself."

I shrug. "I'm taking us to Hawaii. What do you think?"

Now he's back in my face again. This guy is relentless. I glance at Dad.

Savannah calls, "Charlie, I need you over here. I can't run the ship by myself."

Thorwald glares at her, clearly wondering how he can get both of us locked up.

Savannah's dad steps up. "Come on, Lars. Let's go plan out what we do next."

Nolan's dad walks to the door and opens it. "Yeah, Lars, let's figure out our next move in private."

Thorwald snorts and stomps out. The other men stay on the bridge and watch me closely as I take a seat in the captain's chair.

The heavy-set guy steps in front of me, wearing a smirk.

"Do you mind? I'm trying to work here?" I say.

He gives me a dirty look but backs up a step.

I check our position on the VMS and then move across the room to plot it on the chart table. "We've gone about a hundred and fifty miles, more than twenty percent of the way," I tell them.

"Where are we?" says Dad.

I recite the longitude and latitude coordinates. "Right now Hawaii is about seven hundred and fifty miles north of our position," I say. "The VMS will take us straight there. We have enough fuel, so I think we should just keep going."

"Even when Hawaii is so far?" Dad says.

"Seems like the best choice. Problem is, if I take us off the VMS, I'll have to pilot it manually. That would be difficult. I'm not sure I could do that, or even keep us stationary in the water. Plus, I don't know how to set a new course on the VMS once we're off the current one."

"Okay, let's just keep on," Dad says, his voice filled with concern.

I look around. The bridge is full of people, the big men with shotguns, and us kids. Jack and Nolan peer around the adults from the edge of the crowd. It reeks of tension, every adult face looking strained and unhappy.

"Sorry, Dad," I say quietly.

He puts an arm across my shoulders. "Don't be sorry, Charlie," he says with a lopsided smile. "You may have saved our butts." " He turns away and says, "Jack, why don't you go down and ask your mom to bring some breakfast up for you guys?"

Jack hurries out and returns shortly with Mom, who's bearing a tray full of food. I'm sure he's filled her in on everything.

Still, she looks stunned to see me in the captain's chair. "Charlie, what on earth happened last night? Why are you driving the ship back to the U.S.?"

"It's not called driving, Mom. It's sailing."

"Okay, whatever you say, but come over here and eat something."

We walk over to the coffee table, and she lays out breakfast, then says quietly, "What happened?"

"We-lll, it's complicated. But I solved the problem of anybody else getting killed by the zombies. We're too far away for that now."

"I guess so," she says. "Where are we?"

I show her the chart table with our course plotted.

"Still looks like a long way to Hawaii," she says.

"Yeah, it'll be another twenty-two hours or so until we're there."

"Can you take us all the way?"

"Yeah."

"Really?"

"Well, sure. I didn't tell the men this," I say, lowering my voice even more, "but it's really the DPS, the ship's autopilot, that's controlling the ship. The crew had already programmed in a course from Kiribati straight back to Honolulu before they were taken. All I had to do was start up the DPS, and it takes us there. We've been keeping a close eye on all the controls, though, just in case something goes wrong."

"What do you do if that happens?"

"Panic, scream, run around in circles with my arms in the air?" I say. "If we can get close enough to land, we could probably figure out how to get the anchor down."

"Not very reassuring."

"Keep your fingers crossed for the next seven hundred miles. But don't tell anyone else this."

"No, everyone seems to think you're the ship's captain now. It'll be better if they go on thinking you know what you're doing."

I spend the rest of the morning with my butt glued to the captain's chair. People wander in and out. Clearly the word has gotten around the ship about who's in charge, because they seem curious but not surprised to see me there. People are polite but reserved. Some ask questions, most of which I can answer. At some point someone plops a captain's hat onto my head. It feels good.

My dad and Savannah stay with me the whole time.

"I'd like to take a swim and then have a nap in the sun," I say.

"You can't leave. You're on the bridge for good," says Dad.

"Yeah, I know."

By noon or so, I'm done in. I'm more and more sleepy as I sit in the captain's chair.

I wake to find two new and tidy "X"es on the chart table. We've gone almost three hundred miles now. A third of the way to Honolulu.

The sea remains calm as we plow through the waves, moving ever northward. The afternoon drags slowly on. Savannah and Dad remain with me while others drift in and out. I try to remain alert. Almost a full day to go.

CHAPTER 38

Sometime after four P.M. we see an airplane. It's a small floatplane with twin engines. It flies low over the bow.

Jack and Nolan run onto the foredeck and wave and shout. I walk out to one wing of the bridge to look around. All the sunbathers around the pool jump up and down and wave their arms. The pilot must have gotten quite an eyeful.

The plane circles back and flies low over us again this time waggling its wings. They've seen us! After buzzing us, though, it soars up nearly out of sight.

"Keep an eye on it, Savannah."

Jack and Nolan run back in yelling, "They saw us!"

I tell them, "Get your walkie-talkies and go find your dad and Mr. Smith. I think we're going to have visitors."

"I'll go get the launch ready," says Dad.

Just as I'd hoped, the plane comes in low in preparation for a landing on the water nearby.

"Savannah, let me have the pilot's chair."

Leaning forward, I strain to judge their distance and our speed and note which way the wind blows the flags on the bow.

The wind has picked up this afternoon and blows fiercely across the bow.

The plane drones past us, still fifty feet in the air. "They're going too fast to land next to us," I say. A lump comes into my throat, and adrenaline sends needles down my arms. I lift the clear plastic cover from the DPS Emergency Stop button and let my finger hover over the red light. I press the "Full Stop" button. A shiver runs through the ship, and our forward progress slows.

"Where are they, Savannah?" I call to her on the wing.

"They've landed a couple hundred yards behind us and are drifting aft."

"Send the launch," I say and take my sweaty hands from the controls.

"Aye-aye, Captain," says Savannah jauntily and speaks the command into the walkie talkie.

We watch the plane as it rides the waves toward us. Dad and Mr. Smith take the launch over to it and help two figures into the boat. They race back to the ship, while the plane takes off.

The cheering on board echoes even as far as the bridge. Savannah and I high five each other with both hands.

A few minutes later, two Paradise Cruise Lines officers walk onto the bridge. They each carry a duffel bag, from which one of them pulls out a small book and pen. They're followed by our dads and a parade of passengers.

"Charlie, I'd like to introduce you to Captain Oliver and Able Seaman Janek. They're from the cruise line. This is my son, Charlie," says Dad. Both men are fit and young in their crisp white uniforms. Captain Oliver is a tall man with burnished brown skin and alert eyes. Janek, who stands a step behind the

Captain, is around six feet with short, sandy hair and even features. The Captain looks around the bridge and then back at me. His eyes widen slightly as he studies me in the captain's chair. I quickly stand to face him and pull the captain's hat from my head.

"Who's in command here?" he says.

"I am, sir," I reply.

"Where's the crew?"

"Savannah's first mate, Jack's handled the wings, and Nolan the engine room," I say, pointing at each of them in turn.

"Where's the *real* crew?"

"They were infected shortly after we left Mexico, and none of the officers survived."

"Infected with what?"

"One of the crew carried it on board with him and quickly spread it to the rest of the crew members. Most of the passengers were spared."

"Carried *what* on board?" he asks again.

"A zombie infection. It spread rapidly among the crew until most of them were taken."

He looks doubtfully around the room. Luckily, others back me up.

"It sounds insane, I know," says Nolan's dad.

"We didn't believe it either," says Savannah's dad, "until the undead were swarming the ship."

"You don't expect me to believe this, do you?" says Oliver.

"Believe whatever you want, but we've been on our own for six days," says Dad. "Charlie here managed to get us started for home. How did you find us?"

"The Los Angeles Police Department contacted the cruise line. Both the cruise line and the coast guard have been searching for you. Who made that call?"

Nolan raises his hand. "I did."

"What's your name?"

"Nolan Hoskinson."

Captain Oliver looks at me skeptically. "One of your crew?"

"Yes."

"Tell me the circumstances surrounding that call," he says to Nolan.

Nolan tells them about the crew being taken over by zombies and how we went to the island to use the phone. "I spent the whole day on the phone trying to explain and convince someone that we needed help. I wasn't sure they believed me."

"Okay, well . . . I guess it worked. I'm here, aren't I?"

Nolan shoots a triumphant glance at his dad.

The captain says, "Let's put this zombie business aside for now. What's the status of the ship?"

"The communications room was destroyed by fire, but otherwise everything is operational. Here's our position, sir," I say, pointing at the chart before realizing he already knows this." He and Janek step forward and examine the charts carefully.

The captain turns to me and scowls. "What happened to Communications?" he asks.

Jack says, "A zombie attacked us as we were coming from the carpentry shop, so Nolan pushed it in the communications room, and then I firebombed it."

"You what? No, never mind," says the captain.

"There are twelve hundred and fifty-eight passengers and sixteen crew left on board," I say.

He looks up and frowns, then notes this fact in his book.

"All of the sixteen work in the kitchens or dining rooms."

"You used the DPS to keep to the VMS course?" he asks.

"Yes, the crew had entered a course to Honolulu before they were killed."

He nods. "Janek, go below and check out the communications and engine rooms. See if you can find some of those sixteen crew members and have a chat with them."

The captain turns to the crowd. "I need the bridge cleared *now*." He pulls a mobile sat phone from his pack.

I feel like crawling into a hole in the ground. Oh, crap, wonder what they do to mutineers these days.

"Charlie, I need you and your crew to stand by in the lobby there."

Savannah, Nolan, Jack, and I slump on the benches that line the walls. Dad stands next to me.

"Dad, what're they going to do to me?" I ask glumly.

"I think it'll be okay. Just hang in there."

The hands of the clock drag around to dinner time before the captain summons me back onto the bridge.

"Charlie," he says, "am I to understand that you took over command of this vessel and undertook to sail it from Kiribati to Hawaii?"

"Yes. It was my decision. The rest of them really had no choice."

"You removed the officers on duty?"

"Well, no, there weren't any officers left. If I could just explain. We'd been stranded for days in Kiribati. We had no way to communicate with the outside. We tried the satellite phone on Kiribati, but we didn't think anybody would come. I had to do something."

"It's a very serious thing to commandeer a ship, the captain says, his voice harsh. "I think I understand that you were in extreme circumstances." He glances at Janek. "Janek reports that the remaining crew tell a remarkable story that's not inconsistent with what you said," he tells me in a friendlier tone. "Many of the passengers also speak of being saved by a bunch of kids. I think we'll wait for others to sort all this out. As far as I'm concerned, you seem to have stepped in when no one else was able to and saved the ship."

I exhale and look up at him. "Thank you, sir."

"We'll take it from here, Charlie." He shakes my hand with a strong grip.

"Yes, sir. Thank you, sir."

"Why don't you go get some dinner and then come back up and we'll talk," he says. "You can release the rest of your crew. We'll talk to them later."

"Yes, sir."

As I walk out I raise my arms up into the air and exclaim to my gang, "They're not gonna shoot me!"

Savannah and my dad look at me in surprise. Nolan and Jack jump up and give me a high five.

"We're supposed to go to dinner and come back later to talk," I tell them.

I've been on the bridge or in the lobby next door for eighteen hours. It feels good to get out of there. Jack puts my captain's hat back on my head as we walk down to the dining room, hooting and laughing all the way.

It's almost seven P.M., and the dining room is packed. There's a little man in a beret and khaki pants serving as maître d'.

My dad approaches him and says, "Table for five, please."

"There's a forty-minute wait this evening," the little man says, as snooty as in any New York restaurant. Then he spots my hat. He takes a closer look at me and says, "I'm sorry, sir. We can seat you right away."

"Thank you," says my dad.

The maître d' scoops up menus and leads the way. When we're seated, the snooty little dude leans close to me and says, "Would you care for some wine this evening, Captain?" He hands me the wine menu.

I smile and sit up straighter. "Hmmm," I say, looking it over.

"No, he wouldn't," says my dad firmly.

"If I can be of service to you, please don't hesitate to ask," he says, and glides away.

I see there've been some changes to the menu. We have only two choices. Must be the easiest things they can make. A waitress, who looks a lot like one of the girls at our party last night, fills the water glasses and brings us bread. She winks at Jack before she leaves.

"I like the ladies, and the ladies like me," he sings.

"Would the young captain care for a breadstick?" says Nolan in his snootiest voice as he holds out the bread basket, his lips pursed and pinkie lifted.

"Certainly, thank you."

"So, 'Captain,' what did the real captain have to say?" asks Savannah.

"Nothing much. We're supposed to go back to the bridge after dinner and talk."

"What are they going to do?" Dad says.

"They didn't tell me anything. I'm back to being just a kid again."

"I don't think so, Charlie," says Jack, pointing his breadstick behind me.

A soft hand grips my shoulder, and a pair of lips smacks me in the cheek. "You're our little captain!" says the older lady.

"What?" I draw back in surprise.

"I just had to say thank you for saving us." She pats my hand. "Such a brilliant boy! I told Winnie I just knew it was you when I saw the hat. You *are* the captain, aren't you?"

"Uh, not really. There's a real captain on board now."

"Oh, but *you* saved us. We all know how you took us away from that godforsaken island! Oh, my Lord. It gives me the shivers just to think of it."

"Uh, thank you, ma'am," I say, my cheeks hot.

"I've just got to thank these boys, too," she says as she moves over to place a hand on Jack's and Nolan's shoulders. "You two saved my life. I was just about to go down to dinner when you made a special trip to my room."

"We wanted to make sure you were safe," says Jack.

"Aren't you just cute as a button," she says as she pinches Jack's cheek.

"I'll let you eat in peace," she says and gives me one final pat before she leaves.

I'm surprised to see that a line of people has taken her place. The men want to shake my hand. Most of them walk all the way around the table and shake hands with all of us. Each of us gets singled out by certain people as the one who saved them. Savannah gets several hugs. One man promises me free dental care for life and presses his business card into my hand. I stand to greet them, trying to fend off the touchiest of them. My jaws ache from smiling, and I know my face is beet red by the time my dad waves everyone away and the waiter takes our order.

"Oh, Charlie, our little captain!" Jack says in a falsetto voice. Nolan laughs.

"You'll get yours, you little pipsqueak," I say.

"You mean the cute little button over there?" says Nolan.

"Settle down, boys," Dad says. "You've been hidden on the bridge, but the stories have been going around the ship all day. It'll die down."

Mom and Lois come out of the kitchen to say hi.

"You're real heroes, kids, you know that?" says Mom.

"It's crazy," I mumble

"Enjoy it while you can," Mom says. "Lois, why don't you sit with them and eat? You need to rest your legs a little." Mom gives us all a big smile and then heads back to the kitchen.

"Look, there's that big man that caused so much trouble," Lois says, tipping her head toward Thorwald across the room.

"I want to kick him in the nuts. That's what I want to do," I say, remembering how he manhandled me and shoved Dad. I'm still wound up from all the attention.

"Yeah, what this cruise needs is more nut-kicking," says Savannah with a sly giggle.

Lois says, "Kick him in the nuts. Then kick his *wife* in the nuts, too."

Everyone laughs.

CHAPTER 39

After dinner, we go back to the bridge and knock on the door. Janek opens it, smiles at us, and moves aside.

Before I can stop myself I go to the control panels to check our position. Someone clears his throat noisily. Janek gives me a quick shake of the head and then looks at Captain Oliver. The captain leans over the chart table, one hand poised midair, glaring at me.

"'Scuse me, sir." I back away from the captain's chair.

"Why don't you have a seat over there, and the captain will be with you in a moment." Janek gestures at the couch along the wall.

Jack smirks at me as I pull off my hat and sit down. "Guess 'our little captain' was demoted." He elbows Nolan.

Finally, the two men join us. "Kids, we'd like to hear the whole story, from start to finish," says Janek, sitting down with notebook and pen in hand. The four of us look at one another, then I take a deep breath and say, "Well, on day one, I saw Harry get bit by a rat."

"Who's Harry, and what does that have to do with anything?" says the captain.

This will take forever.

It takes three hours. There's silence at the end.

"Holy moly," says the captain. He sounds impressed.

Janek scribbles furiously.

"Did you get all that, Janek?" says the captain.

We laugh.

We're up late talking to the captain. They want to make sense of it all and find out more about the zombies. It's after midnight when we finally fall into bed.

CHAPTER 40

DAY ELEVEN

On our last day, I sleep 'til ten, then get up slowly, still feeling tired.

"What should we do today?" Jack asks.

"I've got a girlfriend to hang out with. I have no idea what you're going to do."

Savannah and I end up lying limply on lounge chairs near the pool. She stares out at the water while I stare at her. Every so often we cool off in the pool together.

Land appears soon after lunch. We pull into Honolulu's harbor just as dusk falls.

Savannah and I go back to our rooms to get cleaned up. I shower and dress, then go up to the bridge and knock on the door. The captain nods when I ask permission to enter the bridge. I watch them as they bring the *Pacifica* into the dock.

It's a lot easier to pilot the ship on an empty ocean compared to docking it. There are some tense moments easing into a slip. Eventually, the ship bumps the dock and shudders to a stop. I cheer, and Janek grins at me.

"That was a tough one," he says.

As I stare at the busy port below us, I realize I'll be back home soon.

"You kids have an amazing story to tell," the captain says, pulling me from my thoughts. "You did a good job, and you saved a lot of lives on this ship."

"Thank you, Captain," I say.

"If you ever want a job, I'll keep a spot open for you."

"What, as a cabin boy?" says Jack, entering the bridge.

"No, as admiral," I say.

"Maybe just a seaman to start," says the Captain.

"I'm sure he wouldn't stay there for long, though," adds Janek.

"No, that's for sure," says Oliver.

"Thank you, Captain, for rescuing us," I say and hold out my hand.

"Thank *you*," he replies, shaking it.

"Best of luck to you, Captain Charles," says Janek.

I give them a playful salute, and after a wistful look around, I leave.

Back in my room, I pack my gear in my suitcase, and go back up on deck. It's nearly empty because most passengers, anxious to leave, line up close to the exits.

I find Savannah leaning on the railing. I stand next to her, and we look out at the city.

"I'll miss you. Will you miss me?" she says.

"Uh, yeah, I guess"

"Charlie!"

"Yes. I *will* miss you." I know it's true. I'll miss her a lot. I wrap my arms around her. "We'll keep in touch?" I ask.

She nods. We kiss and then kiss again.

"Here, Charlie, this is for you." She holds out a small package. I take it. Before I get it open, Savannah is gone.

I open it. There's a card with a note from Savannah. She's made a playlist for me.

"Aw, a bunch of love songs for Charlie," says Jack.

How come, wherever I go, there he is?

I logon using the port wifi, upload the files to my iPhone, and play the first tune. I smile at Jack and give him one of the ear buds. "Thriller" by Michael Jackson beats in our ears. Now I know what Savannah gave me. It's a collection of zombie songs.

THE END

ABOUT THE AUTHOR

Laura Hansen is a scientist, professor, and author. She is currently at work on the next volume of the Zombies in Paradise series. Visit her on the web at www.cruiseoftheundead.com.

14697043R00127

Made in the USA
Charleston, SC
25 September 2012